The Whisper Jar

A Collection of Curious Secrets

Happy Reading!
Carol Jenkins

Published by Morrigan Books
Östra Promenaden 43
602 29 Norrköping
Sweden
www.morriganbooks.com

Editor: Kari Wolfe
Editorial Assistance: Amanda Pillar & K.V. Taylor

ISBN: 978-91-86865-03-0

Cover art by Amanda Pillar © 2011
Internal Layout: Amanda Pillar

First Published October 2011

All stories © Carole Lanham reprinted with permission of the author

Collection © Carole Lanham 2011

The moral rights of the author have been asserted.

All those characters in this publication, other than those clearly in the public domain, are fictitious and any resemblance to real persons, living or dead, is purely coincidental.

All rights reserved. No part of this publication may be reproduced or transmitted in any forms by any means, electronic or mechanical including photocopying, recoding or any information retrieval system, without prior permission, in writing, from the publisher.

The book is sold subject to the condition that it shall not, by way of trade or otherwise, be lent, resold, hired out, or otherwise circulated without the publisher's prior consent in any form of binding or cover other than that in which it is published and without a similar condition including this condition being imposed on the subsequent purchaser.

THE WHISPER JAR

BY
CAROLE LANHAM

AVAILABLE FROM MORRIGAN BOOKS:

HOW TO MAKE MONSTERS
by Gary McMahon

VOICES
Edited by Mark S. Deniz & Amanda Pillar

GRANTS PASS
Edited by Jennifer Brozek & Amanda Pillar

DEAD SOULS
Edited by Mark S. Deniz

THE PHANTOM QUEEN AWAKES
Edited by Mark S. Deniz & Amanda Pillar

REQUIEMS FOR THE DEPARTED
Edited by Gerard Brennan & Mike Stone

SCENES FROM THE SECOND STOREY
Edited by Amanda Pillar & Pete Kempshall

CREEPING IN REPTILE FLESH
by Robert Hood

SLICE OF LIFE
by Paul Haines

SCENES FROM THE SECOND STOREY (Int Ed)
Edited by Mark S. Deniz & Sharon Ring

DEDICATIONS

For my husband

I've placed all of my love, and all of my dreams, and all that I am in you for a long time now, Chris. Bless you for keeping every little thing so well.

Praise for
The Whisper Jar

"Carole Lanham is made entirely out of awesome. *The Whisper Jar* is packed to the lid with dark magic and whimsy, while bearing an ominously old-fashioned touch that might make Edward Gorey feel right at home. It deserves to be ranked as a modern classic."
~ Brian Hodge, author of
Mad Dogs and Picking The Bones

"Every now and then, a collection of short stories comes along that not only brings creepiness to new levels, but reaches in a little deeper and leaves something behind. The stories in *The Whisper Jar* are like that...they stick with you like soft voices in the memory. A great book for a dark and stormy night..."
~ David Niall Wilson, award-winning author of *Deep Blue, This is My Blood,* and CEO of Crossroad Press

"With cover artwork that is gorgeous, writing that is addictive and editing that is impeccable, *The Whisper Jar* is sure to be a hit."
~ The Deepening World of Books

"Carole Lanham's collection reminded me of the best of Steven Millhauser and Ray Bradbury. She's absolutely wickedly good at writing short stories that stay with you long after you've stopped reading."
~ Rhiannon Frater, Dead Letter Award-winning author of *The First Days and Fighting to Survive.*

"I read this mesmerizing book in one sitting. Once I was done with the eponymous first tale, there was no turning back. all the stories just drew me in and I lost myself in a world that was real but not quite so. Always, there is a hint of something fanciful, whimsical, fantastic, wonderful, sensual, dangerous and terrifying."
~ aobibliophile

"Honestly, Flannery O'Conner came to mind when I read the orphanage story 'The Blue Word'. There is a definite moment of grace, and the final path to salvation is nothing short of heart breaking."
~ Kinder Trauma

"Carole Lanham writes in her own carefree but intuitive voice. Audiences will slip into these short stories as easily as they would a warm bath, only to be surprised at how quickly the waters deepen."
~ Conrad Zero, *Suicide Kings and Big Game*

"Steeped in mischief and magic, Carole Lanham's collection is reminiscent of classic Grimm fairy tales, each masterfully honed to a contemporary edge with her wit and the darkest variety of humor."
~ Award-winning author Mike Norris,
Gods of a Prosperous Era

"It's intense... a real page turner."
~ Tangent

"Every story has won its share of acclaim, with each one appearing in a 'best of' collection, winning an award, or receiving a nomination. After reading these stories, I can see why...I found myself so thoroughly engrossed, it's likely to be one of the few collections that I will re-read a number of times."
~ Colin F. Barnes, quill-wielder of short fiction and obsessive novelist. *City of Hell*

"Eerie, surprising, beautifully written, with dark humour and a strange, playful, inventive language."
~ Valentina Benivegna of Valentina's Room

"'The Good Part', about a brother getting bullied by his vampire older sister, was fabulous. I felt a "no, not yet!" moment when I read the last page."
~ Alisa Carter, book editor and author of the new YA novel Shifters

"Surprisingly delicious...The best thing I've read in a while."
~ Delisa Carnegie for *The Creativity Rebellion*

"Entertaining and refreshingly different, combining fantasy, horror and suspense in a way only the Horror Homemaker could...Gave me the creeps."
~ Curtis Hoffmeister, author of *Tasty Goth Chicks, Jade*, and the first book in the upcoming Robert Benoit series *Shrouded in Night*.

"Each story in *The Whisper Jar* is a delight, and the tales are told in Lanham's unique and compelling voice."
~ British horror and fantastical author Cate Gardner, *Theatre of Curious Acts*

Foreword

So, tell me...Have you ever had a Jilly Jally Butter Mint? Or seen a blue word? Do you have a keepity keep, and what do you think of the name Velvet Honeybone for a "werewuff"? There are, of course, cracking good story collections out there that deal with pulse-pounding "things & events", and there are cerebral collections that take eerie ideas to the limit, and then there are those touchy-feely anthologies that max out emotions, BUT...rarely do you see all three areas of appeal handled exquisitely in one author, as in this collection. And simply done. Because somehow the complexities and profundities of a Carole Lanham story get filtered and focused through simple perspectives, leaving you, the reader, the choice of just going with the flow or savoring the underlying depth as far as you dare descend.

Exactly how she accomplishes this necessarily remains an enchantment of her art. It has to be different for each reader, anyway. Great writers do that — create ambivalence that fits a wide spectrum of readers. But I can tell you that one of her gifts is that she can become a perfect child. She can recall her childhood (and yours!) with details that are usually forgotten in adulthood. To wit, charming things like the lace wings of a dragonfly, cigar band rings, and your own breath smoking a mirror. That said she is most definitely a sophisticated adult, well-connected with literary traditions and steeped in period research. It is a remarkable thing to enter the savvy world of a grown-up's education and a broad range of life experiences, and still be in touch with the imagination and vitality of your genesis years.

It is also tempting to regard the persistence of childhood characters as a theme in Lanham's work, but the device is more of a prism through which to filter other themes. She seems fascinated by the margins, the seams, the edges of life — those borders beyond which interesting, compelling and meaningful things happen. This is not a titillation writer frantically pushing shock buttons, but rather a fully-ranged storyteller who uses darkness and magic to connect the dots in life. Childhood characters give her the border she needs to explore innocence and evil, passion and eroticism. The touch in delivering these elements is light and subtle. You can take her as your mood suits. Any story will do. You will find enchantment, disturbing undertones, wry humor, romantic eroticism, intrigue, suspense, and sheer escapism in all of them. Aberrations abound, but they are told with such convincing nonchalance that you simply have to believe them. You fall in love with the characters, and your hopes rise for their quests to succeed even as they descend into consensual madness or impossible dreams or a struggle to survive. Whether they survive and how they survive if they do...well, that's as unpredictable as a coin flip.

Would you like some previews? Glad you asked, because I've just finished going over this collection for a second time, and the wonder of it begs to be shared...

'Whisper Jar': Here is the music of Carole Lanham in a poem. The delightful rhymed couplets of a delightfully playful idea are typical. You need read no more than the title to understand that much. But do unscrew the cap and hear what "ghastly secrets" have been entombed therein. Then broaden the title to include the entire eponymous collection, because they are all ghastly secrets — these stories. Ghastly and puckish and melodic and riveting and erotic and fanciful and sometimes poignant, sometimes funny. And always entertaining.

'The Good Part': Are vampires stories supposed to tease? Well, throw away the rules, if they aren't. This one will take you through all the arteries — so to speak — of that literary tradition. And when you are done with the final twist, you may find yourself in line to donate blood.

'Keepity Keep': For sheer invention and fluid storytelling, it's hard to beat this one. And I am betting you will want to believe every fantasy therein. Believe and, in so doing, open yourself to the rending conclusion. Such a poignant tale. Evoking that commitment from the reader is another of Carole Lanham's special skills. And that gives her the power to create marvelous endings. Scary endings. *Lightning bolt* endings.

'The Blue Word': Nor does post-apocalyptic fiction lie beyond Lanham's pen. In this collection you will find a dark world with a historical feel right out of the most shrouded traditions of mysticism. This story supplies one. Set in the fabled Montségur on a cliff in the Pyrenees, something called Salvation House becomes the backdrop for another softly deceptive tale. You may anticipate endings to your heart's content, but you might want to keep a few backups in mind, because the author will play out all the permutations, and even if you guess the right one, there will be nuances quite beyond plot twists.

'Maxwell Treat's Museum of Torture for Young Girls and Boys': Lanham's range of evoked emotions is inclusive, but they are all here in each story. The predominant tone may be whimsy, or unrequited love, or eerie mystery, or fear, or suspense, or even humor, as in this delightful piece.

'Friar Garden, Mister Samuel, and the Jilly Jally Butter Mints': You'll wonder what triggers imaginings like "children smoking" in Friar garden, which is quite a different thing from puffing cigarettes. In fact, in this playful piece it involves a kind of Truth or Dare ritual, and a shibboleth that summons Dragon Hornets, and — hmmm. No point in trying to describe what needs to be felt. Just beware of what comes of eating Jilly Jally Butter Mints and know that bending concepts and words is another Lanham trademark. She runs them through her reduction valve of youth or fantasy or an unfettered character with a moron IQ, and it all comes out magic! The magic itself often turns from white to black, but with a touch as airy as a puff of wind. And while the rapture in Friar garden is unfolding, we see the delicate bloom of a first love trampled into a tragic ending. Magic to tragic is not inevitable in a Lanham story. You just never know. She may tease you with eroticism, poignant love, innocence cloaked in wry adult glimpses, but — always — the unexpected.

'The Reading Lessons': Here the teasing seductions are done to the whim of a single character who is mad or immature or just plain mischievous. The author's camera points at shadows, silhouettes and reflections in such a sensuous way as to allow the reader to experience forbidden pleasures without acknowledgment. Elegance is never lost. Innocence is never really lost. Nothing is compromised. And yet you may go wherever you dare to go into darkness and eroticism. There will be warnings from the outset of something quite beyond holiness, but I promise you, you will be unable to separate it from a prism of innocence until it becomes a prison of damnation for the characters. You may take that first step of the journey with confidence, even delight at the wry glimpses Lanham gives you of innocence, and when the perfectly tuned notes of a rhapsody deviate into dissonance, you are sure to overlook it, to tell yourself you didn't hear right. And so you go with it until you are caught on the downward slope of something aberrant — an outside force or an outré character. Can you help but follow? The eroticism is sustained; the darkness swift and terminal. You cross the bridge one last time, and...

'The Adventures of Velvet Honeybone, Girl Werewuff': A reprise of the rhymed couplets from the eponymous poem that starts the collection, this bit of music will give you a trip through the forest to grandma's house — just like Little Red — only there are delightful and terrifying images along the way. The Wolf, it seems, is of quite a different kind than the traditional one, and a good deal more lethal. The fun here and the chill are in the language, and thus we find a shadow that licks, and descriptions like this one:

> *"It's eyes swam with Evil like fish in a can*
> *And perhaps in there also, was some trace of a man."*

'The Forgotten Orphan': And will you brave the staircase to the attic of the Asylum for Fatherless Children in this very special story? Because now that they've built a special security door — *a second one* — you may not be able to get back down, especially if you have to deal with nefarious interests. Then again, you may find some surprises at the top of the stairs. Shocks even — definitely shocks — that will reverberate to the foundations of that time-worn building. This closer story to a spectacular collection is my favorite. I want to read the novel of *The Forgotten Orphan* — yes, it should be a novel — and see the blockbuster film — can't have a blockbuster novel without a blockbuster film — because the setup of the characters here is a treat that deserves its own universe. Come to think of it, it is a universe, and thus has all the elements and energy to expand indefinitely.

I should mention that every story herein has been nominated for an award or won an accolade of some kind on somebody's "Best of..." list, but that seems almost an understatement. The whole is greater than the sum of the parts, and here we have the entire nine yards...or, if you will, nine works from a name to watch. Carole Lanham has arrived.

Thomas Sullivan
July 4, 2011
www.thomassullivanauthor.com

Contents

Whisper Jar _____ 1

The Good Part _____ 3

Keepity Keep _____ 27

The Blue Word _____ 49

Maxwell Treat's Museum of Torture for Young Girls and Boys _____ 71

Friar Garden, Mister Samuel, and the Jilly Jally Butter Mints _____ 87

The Reading Lessons _____ 123

The Adventures of Velvet Honeybone, Girl Werewuff _____ 141

The Forgotten Orphan _____ 145

WHISPER JAR

High Cross was a dreadful place before the Whisper Jar.
No touch, no taste went by unseen. No wrinkle, bump or scar.
No one kept their troubles in. They kept their troubles out.
And if you said a quiet word, it echoed in a shout.

One evening, Bitty Martin opened sardines for her sup
And told the jar the evil things she'd done to Old John's pup.
Her whispered words fogged the glass & when the act was done,
She capped the secret good and tight and it was shared with none.

Next day she found her little boy, ashamed and blushing pink.
She gave him one good spank and poured her jam into the sink.
"I don't know what you have done, but put your mouth right here.
Confess your crime to this fruit jar as though it were God's ear."

In due time it was noticed that Bitty kept a room
Filled with empty jars that smelled of plums and fish perfume.
When finally someone asked her why she saved them up like gold,
Bitty told her secret for keeping secrets from getting told.

The handiness of such a jar was noted in a snap.
Soon everyone in High Cross was screwing off a cap
And murmuring of black desires or children that they missed
And stuffing their pain down in this convenient orifice.

No secret was too large, it seemed, to fit in a small jar.
A lie took up no less the space than parts lost in a war.
A corpse would fit, if put in right. Or the true father of a child.
Many might go in at once, if very softly piled.

Soon, everyone kept jars on hand and counted them as dear.
Roger found a candle jar for his great love of beer.
Cookie bought a cookie jar for stowing cookie cravings.
Lucy liked a whipped cream jar to handle her mad ravings.

Miss Ella used a Mason to hide a bloody awl.
Her sister, Easy Mary, much preferred a Ball.
Herbert's jar was darkest blue, his wife's was ruby red.
When Herbert died they emptied his and passed it on to Fred.

A wagon came along one day with buttons and gunpowder.
Doc Bishop's Healthful Whisper Jars sold out within the hour.
For people thought it just as well to pickle every sin
And float them in the same sour brine Regret oft lingers in.

High Crossians enjoyed this life of hidden turpitude,
But jars are just jars, after all, and jars may be removed.
It happened someone stole a jar, or else it was mislaid,
And it was generally decided that a Jar Law must be made.

To keep the secrets safe and sound, a Jar House was erected,
And to keep the house, the strongest man, Big Tom, was selected.
To guard the secrets from all theft and any aimless prying,
They strung a noose up by the cross for anyone caught trying.

And so it was that all felt safe, their secrets soundly kept.
Big Tom watched the Jar House and kept it goodly swept.
But Big Tom was a bumbler when it came to his broom handle
And bumbling, swept the floor too hard, tipping Roger's candle.

The candle clinked the Ball jar and the ruby red, besides.
Splinter! Splatter! Secrets tumbled in dirty secret tides.
Then something Grave and Darkish flooded out the door
As the Whisper Jars of High Cross let loose their potent gore.

THE GOOD PART

The first time my sister did it to me, I was twelve years old and it hurt like Hades, even though she said it wouldn't. "Lie down, Gidion, and don't move. I promise it'll be okay." She put her hand in the middle of my chest as if I would jump up and run. And I might have. I wanted to.

"Good God, your heart," she said. Her eyelids fluttered in a way that told me she wasn't so sure about this whole business, either. When she pressed my wrist against her mouth, it jerked away all by itself. "Hold still, you little oaf." Etta breathed a breath and puffed her bangs, as she often did when discomfited. "Don't be afraid now, Giddy."

The way I see it, this was sort of like asking a fellow to wear a grin while holding out his fingers to be chopped off by an axe. In fact, I might have liked that axe idea better. But she rubbed my wrist so nicely against her face, it did relax me some.

Then she started.

Sad to say, it wasn't fast. Etta was shaking like a scourged man sitting on the pot and I could feel her tears running down my arm. Her teeth didn't want to go in. She tracked my skin up with gnaw marks and this made her real mad. Etta Indian-burned my arm trying to position it just so. "Stupid," she sputtered, "Quit wiggling."

"It hurts," I said.

"You're such a baby, Gidion."

"Am not," I said.

I didn't like it when Etta's skin got all red. Usually I'd get hit then, which would mean I'd start hitting too, and whenever I hit Etta, Pap hit me.

Etta took another bang-fluffing breath and her mouth snapped shut around my wrist. This time, her teeth dug down deep and they popped a vein.

It was a mighty pain, that pain I felt. A pain so big, it jarred me rigid. My legs would have snapped off easy as the fingers on a dry branch, I'm pretty sure, yet inside I was a river. Etta just about tapped me dry, she was so enthusiastic.

When it was over, I wasn't rigid anymore. It felt like my bones had vanished and I'd been turned to empty skin. I sprawled on the floor of the barn, my eyes so blurry hot that the constellations outside the wagon door melted until the whole sky turned white. My pants were wet and I would have shivered, if only I'd had the vim for it. Etta was looking more chipper than in all her sickly fourteen years. Like the sky, she melted to white too, a white so bright I could hardly look at her. Or maybe that wasn't the reason.

She wiped her arm across her mouth, bloodying her sleeve. "Thanks, little brother," she said. "You go on and sleep out here tonight, and by morning, you'll be right as rain."

I wasn't, though. I wasn't ever right again.

It all started three days before, when Pap let a black-eyed

drifter called Mr. Jericho spend the night out in our field. Pap wasn't normally generous but Mr. Jericho claimed to be a friend of Ernest Stump, and Ernest Stump was a name old Pap hadn't heard since the war. What I couldn't figure out was this: if poor dead Stump was in the war with my grandfather, how could someone as young as this Jericho fellow possibly know the man? Pap said the drifter was privy to all manner of personal facts that were too intimate to doubt. This being the case, he had a Phlegm-cutter with the man, gave him the blanket off his own bed, and whistled as Mr. Jericho went off to settle in the alfalfa.

Etta and I had a window in our bedroom that looked out over the farm. That night, we sat knee to knee on the sill, speculating about our visitor. "Pap should have chased him off," I said. There was something about the man that deeply troubled me. Why couldn't anyone else see he looked at us like white tail bucks itching for a bullet? "He's got Remington eyes."

"They are nice," Etta sighed and my head just about spun off my neck.

"Nice? They aren't nice at all, Etta. We best lock the doors tonight."

Etta laughed. "That man is the most beautiful man I have ever seen."

I snorted at this. "Men aren't beautiful."

She stared out the window like his beauty had set him glowing so bright, she could spot him across the fields through the oily black of night. "That one is beautiful."

Etta was born two months early and that was the reason she was so puny. Our Mama barely survived her. She didn't survive me, as it turned out, though I popped out healthy as a horse. Etta spent most of her life in bed, but she was a restless creature. As a rule, she visited the outhouse several times during the night, so I didn't think much about it when she went missing on the night of Mr. Jericho. I was tired and forgot all about our suspicious guest. Later, I learned Etta had visited him. When morning came, I couldn't wake her. Her skin was an unsettling shade of blue.

Fearing she'd gone up to Heaven, I dumped a chamber pot of water on her head to revive her, an act she swore never to forgive me for regardless of how I'd filled the pot. After that, Etta turned a vital pink. That same pink stuck around long after Mr. Jericho took leave of our farm.

It was only a couple of days later that Etta asked me for my blood. "He did something to me, Gidion. I'm different now."

I didn't want her different. She was complicated enough as it was, but most times I could figure her out if I was patient and interested enough to try. Etta was pretty much my whole life. Her and Pap. We didn't hardly do nothing that our elbows weren't bumping together. We were just that miserably close. Other than my friend Samson and my one true love, May Givens, Etta and Pap were about the only people I even knew, unless you counted the ghost of Eloise who also lived with us.

Eloise was my grandmother; a fussy, door-slamming dead woman with a peculiar sense of humor. I had never met the woman, in life or otherwise, except through old Pap's rantings. Old Pap argued with her from sun-up to sun-down, and I could only imagine she was a rascal of sorts, the way she was always using up the last of the toilet paper or leaving a pot to boil over. If you asked Pap, he'd tell you she ate supper with us every night. Sometimes, when Pap had his back turned, she burned the beans, she was such an ornery spirit.

Even though you couldn't rightly call us the most regular of disciples, I suppose I ought to mention the congregation of Fireside Church of God, too. I knew those folks well enough to shake their hand every week and bring them fry bread or Apple Treat when they were sick in bed. But mostly, I went to services to see May. I was going to marry May, except she didn't know that then, seeing how I'd been keeping the news a secret since I was about five. May was as sunny as the sun every day and that sort of sunniness must be infectious because, whenever I was around her, it felt like my insides were yellow with sunshine. Also, she could eat more pie than any boy. I used to compete with her in a contest every year at the Wichita County Fair, but, after three failed attempts, I made up my mind to accept the uselessness of it. The best thing about May was that she was the Reverend Given's daughter, and it was also well-known the Reverend made a point of visiting any parishioners he hadn't seen in church for a spell. I know you're not supposed to be rewarded for back-sliding, but I was because, whenever the Reverend rode out to the farm, his daughter came, too.

Still, a church, four people and one ghost ain't many people to know and, of them all, I guess Etta was around the most.

"I'll kill him," I said of Mr. Jericho after he turned her odd. Etta just shook her head.

"Can't," she said.

"Well, I could try."

"He's long gone from here, Gid, but that don't matter anyway. What matters is I'm changed and there ain't no going back. If you don't let me sip some of your blood, I'm going to have to kill someone."

Gosh. A week before, I'd have laughed myself blue over those same words, but I could see she was different now. She'd killed a squirrel the night before. What she really craved though, was human blood. "You can't want

THAT," I protested.

"Can," Etta said.

"How would anyone as small as you overpower a big fellow and kill him?"

"I'm strong now, Gidion. Look..." And she lifted me up like I was a bride. Of course, I wasn't too big as yet myself, but still, Etta had long since been excused from carrying milk pails, she was such a frail girl. "I could lift Pap too, iffin' he'd let me."

I thought I might be sick. "It ain't right, Etta."

"Well, it is what it is, Gidion. Now, are you gonna let me have some of your blood or ain't you?"

"Are you crazy?"

Etta shrugged. "Okay, but don't blame me when the Widow Jenkins doesn't wake up tomorrow morning."

"Huh?"

"Never mind. She's just an old grouch anyway. I'd be doin' everyone a favor."

"You stay away from that old woman," I warned.

"As I said, that's up to you."

I didn't let her drink my blood, though. It was too horrible. "Where are you going?" I asked when she got up in the middle of the night.

She looked at me with weird eyes. "You know exactly where I'm going."

I grabbed her arm. Etta wrestled it away like nothing.

The next evening, Reverend Givens and May rode up in their brand new Sears runabout. "Have you heard the news?" May said, sniffling in a hanky. "Mrs. Jenkins died last night."

My legs felt like they'd been turned to soup and I collapsed in a kitchen chair.

An hour later, Etta whispered a secret in my ear. "Samson is next."

I let her have my blood.

The first time we had to change was after our drummer's wagon ran off the road in the rain. It was a fancy thing, that wagon, with gold-gilt doors and an Egyptian pyramid painted on the wood. A man with no arms did the pyramid for my father as payment for some bootblacking. He stuck a paintbrush between his teeth and wiggled out a pyramid prettier than any two-armed man could manage. He told my father that such a romantic image would bring us good luck, and it did. For a while. We sold more suspenders than anyone this side of the Missouri, or so that's what we told folks.

Then came the day it rained like hell. I was sitting up front with my father when we hit a rut and flew off in opposite directions. Etta stayed in the wagon, tossing with cigars and buttons and toothpicks. Afterward, Vamoose, our horse, had a twisted neck. Father's was twisted, too. Etta and I brushed ourselves off, kicked aside a few dozen spilled buttons, and were otherwise fine, but Father was dead.

One day later, Pap drove in from a place called Hope, Kansas to bury his only son. "I'll have to make you into farmers now," he said. The old man always said it took a God-awful amount of work to change us from citified folk into farmers. That wasn't half as bad as the changing Mr. Jericho did to Etta, though.

We didn't know what to call it, this bad thing that took over our lives. Blood-Digging was what I named it inside my head. I was so ashamed that I couldn't mouth a solitary word about it to God, even when I was saying my prayers. I kept to the easier sins instead. Etta always told me if you looked real hard, you could find the good in just about anything, but I couldn't see what could possibly be good about this. I hoped that Etta had satisfied her craving at long last and wouldn't crave blood no more.

But she did. Worse than before.

The next time it happened, we were in bed and I was pretending to be asleep. "Quit it, Gidion."

I didn't open my eyes, though.

"It has to be done, little brother. You wanna sleep through it, go right ahead."

Tears tried to squirm out from under my eyelids. The last time she'd done it to me, it made me sick for a whole day, and still, that wasn't enough blood to make her not want blood anymore. Would Etta drink me dry before she stopped wanting blood so bad?

I pressed my jaw against my collarbone to keep her from doing it but Etta just tilted my head back up and helped herself. Meantime, I was still "asleep".

"It's alright, Giddy," she whispered. "I won't drink as much this time."

And this was true enough. I was a little wobbly the next day, but I wasn't sick like before. It was my soul that suffered this time. It sat in the bottom of my stomach like a swallowed rock.

That night, I acted like I needed to watch out for our pregnant Guernsey and slept out in the barn.

"What's it feel like when I'm drinking it, Gidion?" Etta asked me the next day after Pap took off for town. I was ready to bolt and make my escape, but Etta grabbed my arm. Her fingers didn't even seem like fingers, they stopped me so good. "Does it hurt when I drink your blood?"

I stared down at that hand, knowing I couldn't twist away if I tried. "What do you think, Etta?"

She slid me across the floor like a hound on a leash trying to hold his ground with his toenails. "Are you shaking, Gidion?"

"I better get to work."

"Does it feel good when I do it?"

I chewed up my lip like it was meat. "I don't like it, Etta."

She used to say the two of us were really all alone in life, because Pap was old and wouldn't be around forever, but the good part was that we had each other. You might think that she'd feel guilty about all this bad Blood-Digging, but she only laughed her head off. "You little liar," she said.

On my thirteenth birthday, Etta suggested making me like her. "I thought I already was like you," I said.

"Don't be stupid. You're just food. But I could make you like me. I think I know how Mr. Jericho did it."

"No, thank you," I said.

"Are you sure? Because the way you are now is pretty pathetic."

"If you so much as try, Etta, I'll never let you near me again."

Etta's face turned red as a strawberry. "Fine."

Pathetic as I was, Etta liked having me handy. She could throw me easy as a pillow, but I had that much going for me, at least. It struck me that she must need me to say yes before she could make me into a Blood-Digger. While this seemed as good a news as I was ever apt to get, by now, I'd come to the realization I couldn't keep her from killing people no matter how much I let her drink. Something was wrong with me that I didn't turn her in, I guess. But who was I supposed to turn her in to?

She'd have killed that lantern-faced Sheriff Wagstaff who kept the peace in Hope by smiling big at people. Etta said I was saving lives every time I let her have my blood, like Jesus on the cross. Of course, I could only be like Jesus every other day; otherwise, I would have dried up like a creek.

It was her habit to do it to me three times a week. We slept in the same bed so there was nothing to stop her. "What if Eloise sees us?" I asked once, thinking Etta might not like the idea of that.

"You don't believe in Eloise."

"She might be real," I allowed.

"If she is, she must like to watch because she ain't breathed a word of it to Pap."

Pap was clueless, it was true. I probably could have grown a third arm and the man wouldn't have noticed. I reckon he loved us well enough, he just didn't pay us very much mind.

On my fourteenth birthday, Pap surprised us. He said we were getting too big to sleep in the same room. "A sixteen year old girl needs her privacy," Pap said.

It felt like he'd cut a chain off me. We'd have to build a new room onto the house but, with any luck, we could have the job done by winter.

"I should have noticed how big the two of you are getting," Pap said. He looked off in the vicinity of the pothook, and the kettle seemed to swing a bit. "What do you say, Eloise? Is it time to split these two kids up?"

A tingling started in my veins, and the tingling turned to panic.

Etta was dipping candles at the hearth. "I'd like to get away from that stinky old boy. You have no idea what it's like for me, Pap."

I looked at Etta, more surprised by her words than I was by my tingling.

"He leaves his underclothes all over my things."

Pap laughed.

Etta grinned. "So, when can I take over your room, Pap?"

"My room?" Pap said.

"Well, you don't expect me to wait for you to make the house bigger, do you?"

Pap was predictably outraged. "I ain't giving you my room and I ain't building another one neither. Have a care where you put your underclothes, Gidion. I'm an old man. I can't be building a bigger house at this time in my life."

When she climbed in bed that night, Etta was twirling a pair of my unmentionables around her finger. "I guess you're stuck with me, little brother."

May Givens was one year older than me and, at fifteen, practically a woman. I began attending church regularly, in part to redeem my soul, in bigger part to see May. Etta never went along and the best minutes of my week came directly after services. May would walk over to Pap and ask about the farm. Sometimes we'd take a walk and Pap would shuffle along behind to let us be alone.

When we were little, May used to stamp on my foot or kick me in the shins, behaving as though she thought I smelled. Not anymore. I liked May and she liked me. I could tell. For one thing, she never kicked me no more.

"I only did that because you looked so cute when you got mad," May confessed when once I dared to remind her about all that foot-stamping of old.

"Really?"

"I'm just surprised you don't hate me, Gidion."

"Oh," I said. "I don't hate you. I never did."

May had long, light brown hair and sometimes the little curls on the end would tickle my elbow when we walked.

"I reckon kicking is just a little girl's way of kissing," she said. Her curls brushed my arm, giving me goose bumps.

"Then I wish you'd kick me now," I blurted.

May giggled at that. "If Pap wasn't looking, maybe I would."

I had a brave moment just then and pulled her behind a big tree. "Go on then," I told her breathlessly, and I looked down at my shin, waiting for her to do it.

She didn't kick me, though. She kissed me on the forehead. "Gosh, May," I said, my cheeks fire-hot.

She tickled me with a curl. "Gidion Lloyd, you're about the sweetest boy I know."

Etta put her hand on my thigh. "Tonight we're going to try something new."

I closed my eyes.

"Your veins are starting to get wormy, so I've picked out a new one right here." She fingered a spot at the top of my leg.

I sucked in my breath. "Maybe we shouldn't, Etta."

When I opened my eyes, her face was red. "Okay, Gidion," she said. She drug her nails over my knee, down to my ankle bone, leaving a streak of scratches.

I pretended that it didn't hurt. "You could try my wrist," I offered.

Etta shook her head.

"My neck then."

"No."

I felt it again, that lightning bolt of panic zigzagging

through my veins. "Come on, Etta."

"Do you want me to do it, Gidion?"

"Whatever you want," I said.

Etta puffed her bangs. "I asked you what you want."

Etta never usually asked what I wanted. "I know you need it, so just go on."

Etta stared at me with her weird cold eyes.

I thumped the artery in my neck like I'd seen her do on countless occasions. "I'm not wormy no more. See?"

Etta didn't move.

"What are you waiting for?"

"I guess I don't need it."

I licked my lips. "But I don't mind."

"Just go to sleep, Gidion." She laid down with her back to me.

"You're not going to do it tonight?"

"Nope."

"Tomorrow, I guess?"

"Maybe."

Once, when I was four or five, I had a fever seizure. I had one again, right then and there, only I don't think I had a fever.

"Are you alright, Gidion?" Etta asked, rolling over to have a look at me.

My teeth were clacking like a baby rattle. "Maybe, just this once, you could use my leg," I said.

Samson Piebald used to be fat, but he grew up like a string bean. He was the tallest fellow I knew and, to his way of thinking, I was the unluckiest. For as long as I could remember, Samson was sweet on Etta. "Poor old Gid," he liked to say. "God gave him the prettiest girl in all the world to live with, and she's his own dern sister."

He'd cackle and slap his knee, as if it got funnier the more times he said it. The older we got, the more times he said it.

"Why don't she never smile at me, Gidion? I smile at her all the time."

"Etta don't smile," I said.

Samson and I were setting a trap for Eloise, a favorite past time of ours. This one involved a ball of twine, some bacon grease, and the Holy Bible. Samson tied a length of twine around the doorknob and ran his hand through his yellow hair. "Hey, Gid, did you ever see Etta in the all together?"

I made a face like I might lose my lunch on the top of his head. At that moment, I was standing over him in the middle of the supper table. "Shut up, Sam, you big pig."

Samson fiddled with his knot. "Well, will you tell her I like her at least?"

"Tell her yourself," I said as I wrapped my end over a rafter.

"I can't. I love her so much, she makes me shy."

"Shoot, Samson. Etta thinks we're still kids wearing knickers and playing marbles. I don't reckon she'd be interested in you."

"Kids?" Samson said, giving the twine a snap to test it. "That's a laugh."

"Ain't it though? Pass me that lard, will you."

Samson hung his head in woe. "You have no idea how much it hurts to love that woman, Gidion."

"If my family invited you and Pap to a picnic after church, would you come, Gidion?"

I was playing with a violet I'd picked in the churchyard, but I couldn't quite figure a way to give it to

May without letting Pap see. "We'd come," I told her, even though I was pretty certain Pap would hate the very notion of it.

"Next Sunday then? If it rains, we'll eat lunch on my porch."

"That'd be nice," I said. I thrust the violet out to her, though Pap rolled his eyes at me.

May smiled and touched it to her nose and kicked me playfully.

"A picnic with the Reverend?" Pap snorted when I got up the nerve at suppertime to ask him about it. "I can't think of a thing I'd less like to do."

"Aw, come on, Pap. Just do it for me."

"I already put on uncomfortable clothes and go to that sasafrassin' church for you. What more will you ask of me, boy?"

Etta was picking at her stew. "Why do you want to go on a picnic with Reverend Givens anyway, Gidion?"

"He don't want to go on a picnic with Reverend Givens," Pap snarled. "He wants to go on a picnic with that daughter of his, May."

"Is that true, Gidion?" Etta asked.

"I guess so."

"You like May Givens?"

"It's just a picnic," I said, chewing up my peas in a casual-like way.

Etta slammed her fist on the table and everything from the plates to me hopped up in the air. "I'll go with him, Pap," she brightly declared.

I coughed out a pea. "May invited Pap."

"Oh, I don't mind. Someone's got to keep the two of you from kissing behind the bushes." Naturally, Pap was

17

willing to surrender that job to Etta.

"Alright," I agreed. "But you have to take Samson."

Etta coughed out a pea herself. "Samson Piebald? That big old lumpy sack of flour?"

"He ain't lumpy no more," I assured her, but she looked so sizzling mad, I figured I'd gotten even.

We spread three blankets on the river bank and piled them high with food. May's brothers ran around terrorizing the ducks while the Reverend grilled me about my plans for the future. "I'll keep working the farm like I always have," I said, wiping my mouth on a napkin that had a fancy little cross embroidered in the middle.

"It's a family enterprise," Etta explained. "We'll work that land till the day we die. Right, Gidion?"

"I reckon," I mumbled. "This cobbler sure is something, Mrs. Givens."

"We've built a good strong house too," Etta went on to elaborate. "It's small and Gidion and I have to double up, but we like it just fine."

"Double up?" the Reverend's wife asked.

"In bed," Etta said, loud and proud as you please. "We're thick as thieves." And she gave her nose a healthy honk inside that pretty napkin.

"That's a little queer," Samson interjected.

Thinking fast, I asked May if she'd like to take a walk along the river. Etta was thinking fast, too, and said she and Samson would come along.

My sister walked between May and I the whole way, intent on being an obstacle. But, while Etta was helping load a hamper into the buggy, May gave me a little kiss. It was short, I guess, but I re-lived it so many times right after, it stretched into one long never-ending kiss.

I didn't know a girl's lips could be so soft. Etta's weren't. I wondered how those lips would feel pressing against my wrist.

"Wouldn't it be swell, Gidion, if you married May some day and I married Etta?" We were having a game of mumblety-peg and Samson was in a wildly dreamy mood, considering he was losing. "Just think of all the fun we'd have."

I threw my knife, wishing with all my heart Etta would take a sincere interest in Samson. Then I felt horrible about that wish. Since the beginning of the game, Samson had been playing reckless. This was the third time he'd had to brace his chin against the dirt and pull his peg out with his teeth. Watching him struggle, I decided I wouldn't wish Etta on my worst enemy.

Samson spit out his peg. "Do you really sleep in the same bed with her every night, Gidion?"

I pitched my knife but blew the throw. "It ain't as good as you think, Samson."

"I find that hard to believe," he said.

Later, I was brushing Vamoose II when Etta came up on the threshing floor and gave me a look I usually only saw in the dark. "Come away from that horse," she said.

I set aside the brush.

"Move up against the wall."

I did.

"I need you, Gidion. Do you need me?"

I turned my face and arched my neck.

Etta grabbed my mouth and turned me so I was looking her dead in the eye. "Do you, Gidion?"

The insides of my cheeks were pressed together, right to left. "Let go," I said in a squished voice.

She dropped my face. "You're fifteen years old today, Gidion. What do you want for your birthday?"

I shrugged.

"Do you want me to suck your blood?"

I picked up straw off the floor with my toes. "Iffin' you want to."

"Stop it, Gidion. Stop acting like it's all me."

"It is all you, Etta."

For the first time in forever, she didn't turn red when I said something she didn't want to hear. She was just plain turnip-white. "Why then, you must want me to leave you alone, I guess?"

I felt that old panic brewing in my blood, yet I nodded my head yes.

"You want that giggly May Givens?"

I squinted at her. If I said yes, would she hurt May? Etta was a killer, after all. But I never could lie convincingly. "I intend to marry her when I turn sixteen."

"Then it's time for this to end between us," she said, and she left me leaning against the wall, breathing hard, like I'd just run a race.

She made a pallet for me in the corner with barely straw and a piece of flannel, and the good part is she actually treated me pretty nice after that. And the next Sunday, I got to kiss May again, because Pap waited in the wagon.

The kiss was longer this time and I liked it so much, I grabbed her and hugged her and twirled her around. She even brushed her lips against my neck, or maybe that was an accident. I put my hand on the back of her head and smashed her mouth against my skin until I could feel her tongue and teeth. May liked it so much she started to moan.

Then she hit me. "What are you doing?" she cried.

"Holding you," I said.

"Well, I don't like it. Not here."

"Where then?" I asked her anxiously.

She put her hand on my forehead. "You're sweating like a pig, Gidion. I thought you were a nice boy."

"I am," I said, but she was right. I was far too sweaty. "I just like you, May."

"I like you too," she said, smiling at me again. "No harm done, I guess."

I sighed with relief. "Can I see you next Sunday?"

"Of course," she said. "But let's bring Pap next time."

I hated the pallet and yet, Etta kept her word and left me alone like she said she would. I got my very most evil wish too, because she started seeing Samson. I saw them walking hand in hand around the farm sometimes. We used to be that way. "Watch your step, Giddy," she'd say, if it happened to be muddy. "Hold on to me, Giddy, so I don't lose you," she'd boss, when we were in the city. "It's just you and me now, Giddy," she'd whisper, when we were lying in bed and feeling scared of our cranky new Pap.

Now, I would stay wide-eyed all night, listening to her roll this way and that in our old bed. Sometimes, I touched the place on the inside of my leg where a couple of bumpy scars marked the flow of my blood. I'd press those two bumps hard enough to feel my blood moving inside of me. It felt like my veins were glutted.

Meantime, I no longer reached for May's hand when we walked. It was safer that way.

She used to wait for Samson after dinner in the barn. One night, the last and worst night of them all, I went to see what they were doing, but Samson wasn't there. Etta smirked when she caught me standing on a wash tub under the window peeking in the barn. I was so startled, I slipped and she caught me. Once I got my balance, she started to take her hand away, but I curled my fingers and held on hard.

"What's wrong with you, Gidion?" Etta wanted to know.

"I miss you, Etta."

"Why? Where did I go?" She pulled her fingers free and wiped them on her dress.

"You never talk to me no more."

"You wanna talk?" Etta said. I nodded. She waited.

I cleared my throat. "That Mr. Jericho...he ruined us good, I think."

"What do you want, Gidion?" She headed back inside the barn and I followed at her heels.

"I want things to be the way they used to be before he came along."

"Well, they can't be," Etta said.

There was a time when Etta considered it her greatest duty to cheer me up. In return, I'd lather mud in my hair and work it into a rooster comb if it would raise her spirits. Now, all she'd give me was the back of her stiff shoulders as she hurried on her way.

"I want you to need me, Etta," I said.

Etta threw me a surly look. "What about May?"

"Well..." I said. "I still like her."

"Go away, Gidion. You wear me out with all your stupid hypocrisy."

"What sorta word is that? 'Hypocrisy'?"

"Hypocrisy is being in love with the Reverend's daughter on Sunday morning, and wanting your sister to drink your blood on Sunday night."

"Oh." I stared down at my dirty feet. "I wish I knew what to do."

"Sorry you're so confused, little brother." She started to leave me again.

I grabbed her hand. "I want it," I whispered.

Etta smiled a hard-as-nails smile and waited to hear more. "Anywhere you like, Etta, just, please, do it."

She poked my shoulder, pushing me, backing me up against the wall of the barn. "You want it now?"

"Yes," I croaked.

Using the tip of her finger, she moved my hair off my neck. Her tongue touched me when she spoke. "May can't never make you feel this way. You know that don't you, Gidion?"

My knees seemed as though they might give out. I couldn't wait. I grabbed Etta and pulled her teeth in me.

It was a mighty pain. A terrible, wonderful, white-hot pain. It was blinding how good it felt. Later I was sure to wallow in self-doubt, but while Etta was drinking my blood, I was in a place where I didn't have to think. That place was the only place to hide anymore.

I've tried to picture what Samson saw when he came into our barn. He wouldn't have guessed that Etta had her teeth in my vein because he'd probably never heard of such things before. Etta hadn't taught him, yet. He'd have thought it was a kiss. He'd have seen my arms wrapped around her, pulling her against me, holding on for dear life. He'd have thought it was something less than it was.

He let out this horrible gargle of a noise. "Ugggck."

But I couldn't stop Etta. Didn't want to, as mortified as I was. Matter of fact, I was more irritated with Samson for interrupting things. We locked eyes over Etta's shoulder. "Laws, that's sick!" he said.

Etta let me drop to the floor and leapt on top of Samson. From where I fell, I saw the bottoms of his shoes as his feet began to kick. I wanted to tell her to stop, but I could never speak for several minutes after Etta did her Blood-Digging. I was on my belly reaching out to Samson, but it was useless. By now, he was making awful sounds and I felt more angry than afraid for him. Etta was supposed to be drinking my blood. Not his.

When his feet quit kicking, I knew he was dead. Etta killed him! And I watched like a fool while she did it.

Afterward, she climbed to her feet and pointed her finger at me, moving like a drunkard. "It's your fault," she said. "I didn't want to do that."

Inside myself, I argued fiercely with those awful words. She hollered, "He was supposed to meet me here tonight. You distracted me!"

I pounded my fist on the floor. Etta ignored this. "From the beginning, you've wanted to play the victim, and I let you. I let you get away with it. Even though you were there every night with your heart pumping and your wrist laid out on my pillow in such a way, you might just as well have tied a bow around it. You acted like I was forcing you, when all along, you wanted me to force you." I hammered on the floor again and Etta stepped on my hand. "I knew you wanted it so bad, you could hardly think on anything else, Gidion, but I let you lie to yourself." She jerked the hem of her skirt free from Samson's leg. "It's that same bad lie that killed Samson here."

"Go to Hell," I finally managed.

"Oh, I will, brother. I wouldn't dream of leaving you

now, after all we've been through together."

I rolled my forehead on my arm. "I wish you'd kill me too."

Etta squatted down next to me and pulled my head up by my hair. "I got bigger plans for you, Giddy."

"No," I said.

"Yes, Gidion. The lies end now. I'm going to turn you like Mr. Jericho turned me."

"I won't do it," I told her. "Why would I ever want to?"

"I'll tell you why," Etta said. "Because I got something on you, Gidion."

I saw *her* then; her sunny smile stained cherry pie-red. Her lips as soft as Heaven... "May," I choked.

"It sure would be a tragedy if you killed off two loved ones in the very same night," Etta said.

I let my head drop on my arm, sick with defeat.

There was no stopping Etta by this point. I sprawled there on the floor of the barn. Waiting. Trying not to look at Samson. In a few minutes, it would be over forever and I could hardly let myself think about it.

One minute. Two minutes. Three minutes...

Fingers sharp as the fan of a rake stretched my eyelids open. Etta had returned.

"Is it done?" I asked.

"Yes, you coward."

Using the tip of her finger, she painted a sticky heart in the middle of my cheek. "She's dead, Gidion."

It might be hard to understand, but the way I look at it, in order to save my beloved May, more people would've had to die. I didn't want Etta to kill May, but I couldn't let myself be turned. If that happened, I'd have had to kill folks every night too, so I'm not sure the end would have justified the means. The good part is (and there's always a good part), Etta doesn't have anything on me anymore. Now I don't love anyone.

Except for her.

Keepity Keep

It all begins and ends with a leather book, twenty-five significant pages asmudge with jelly thumbprints, pasted valentines, and knee blood. Childhood, if you will, saved on wrinkled paper. You know the stuff: the feathers you collected, the cigar ring the neighbor kid slid on your finger behind the snowball bush, that snotty smear that was once a frog's heart...KEEPSAKES. That's what the front of the leather book says, written in curly gold letters more flowery than flowers. Real gold letters, probably, and worth a small fortune each. Be it a shoebox, a hope chest, or a dresser drawer, one should always have a place to keep what must be kept.

The Turnbull brothers had a leather book.

Sure, a blue birthday candle had been taped in there, but the book held secret keepsakes too, ones even the brothers didn't know about. The apple juice, for instance, that ran off the oldest one's chin when he was pasting a dragonfly wing on Page Three. He didn't see it, didn't mean for it to splat there next to that little green wing. It got kept the same as everything else and much later, when the splat turned yellow-brown, everyone speculated about what it was. Why was it there? Who, they wondered, would keep a stain next to something as marvelous as a dragonfly wing?

Gage was his name, the one who was so sloppy with his apple eating, but Alban, the younger boy, dribbled things, too. A sneeze once, though we'll not delve deeper into the particulars of that. Two drops of paint the color of sulfur. Spit from a kiss. And a full spring shower's worth of raindrops, courtesy of the night he left the book on the windowsill. The point being: some things we save on purpose. Others aren't kept by choice. Either can leave a splotch.

The story of Alban and Gage is about the importance of caring for our keepsakes, both the pearls of youth we choose to save on purpose, and the sneezes that sneak along for the ride. Page One begins in the garden, the day they first met Petaloo.

The Turnbull brothers, like most all brothers, were inclined to make things up. You might think they made up Petaloo, as well. That's fair. Heaven knows, there were a lot of games that belonged solely to them. *Nose Pins* was theirs. *Mipply Pipply* and *Bite the Hook*, but they're not recommended. Likewise, numerous inventions crowded their nursery walls. The *lint-fetcher* was a fine one. The *shirt-buttoner* was not. In any case, both boys were pretenders (fibbers?) and clever (sneaky!) enough to make up just about anything.

On the day they caught Petaloo having her bath in a leaf, Uncle Geoff dropped off the leather book as sort of a *Sorry-I've-Been-Ignoring-You-While-I'm-Off-Seeing-The World* gift. The book was new back then. No stains. No smudges. Just page upon page of clean, ice cream colored paper waiting for something to keep. Then came the leaf.

There aren't many lads with the fortitude to look away from a girl in her tub, so let's not blame them for that. Like the missing tip of Gage Turnbull's second to last finger, seeing her was a sloppy accident. At nine, Gage was clumsy and a little bit round, still waiting to fit his height to his weight. Alban, a year younger, was trim as a willow whip and a great deal more graceful. He ran with the book into Daisy Chain Garden simply because Gage wanted so badly to see it. They hopped over Nipple Rock without incident and tore the heads off an entire patch of pinks, one boy chasing after the other, calling him dirty names. It was the roots of the hornbeam that ended things. Down went roly-poly Gage, bringing Alban along like a tapped domino. Off flew the book. It landed in the cuckoo flowers and a startled "Smeck!" escaped Gage's lips when he peeled back a bloom and saw Petaloo.

Smeck is another Turnbull invention and not the sort that picks lint out of your bellybutton. *Smeck,* in all likelihood, is the most satisfying curse the world has ever known. For one thing, a boy can get by saying it almost anywhere at any time on any occasion because, until now, there has only ever been two people alive who know just how evil a word it is. For another thing, it is highly flexible in that you can combine it with other curses to make it even worse, like *bloody smeck* or *smecking hell.* Alban once told their cranky neighbor, Mr. Dangerbottom, to "go straight to smeck" and he didn't even get a lash for it. *Smeck* was the handiest thing the boys had ever dreamed up. It was also the first human word ever spoken directly to Petaloo. "Would you look at that!" were the next to follow.

There, in the crook of a feltwort leaf, splashing under a drop of dew, was the teeniest girl they'd ever seen. Her hair was longer than she was tall and the same green as the feltwort. Her eyes were two pinpoints of sunlight with a violet smeck in the middle.

I mean, speck.

Of course, she had wings. This was why there was such confusion over what sort of bug she might be. Alban thought a cross between a firefly and a Mayfly. Gage claimed her for a freak beetle. It wasn't until she stood up that they understood she was a miniature girl in every little way. "Holy smeck!" said they.

"I want her," Gage declared right off. "I found her first. That makes her mine."

"You can't keep a girl," Alban said, as he dabbed at the blood running down his scraped shin. "What would you do with her anyway?"

"Put her in a jar and stare at her."

"If that's as creative as you can be, you don't deserve her at all."

"I could make a saddle for Alistair so she can ride him like a horse." Alistair was their three-legged titmouse.

"Alistair would tip over."

Gage scratched his head. "I know! I could let her swim naked in a soda cap on my dresser."

"Now you're thinking," Alban said. Their plans took on delicious life then. "Make her dance on my hand," someone suggested. "Examine her thoroughly for the sake of science..."

"Science?" a little voice said. "I don't like the sound of that."

In perfect synchronicity, Alban and Gage looked at one another and plumbed their ears with their fingers, certain they'd not heard what they'd heard.

"Did she just speak?"

"I think so, yes."

"Maybe it was a bee?"

"No," the voice said, a little bigger this time. "It was ME."

Alban looked closer. "What the devil?" he said. "Are you a bad omen?"

"I don't think so. I'm Petaloo."

"What's a Petaloo?" Alban asked.

She giggled at this. "Don't you know a Wingwee when

you see one?" Goodness, what squeaky little snorts she made! "Hand me my *Dress Upon* from the stem there, will you? And tell me this, if you will; what in the fantong is a *smeck*?"

They blushed to hear a girl say such a coarse thing. "Don't," they cried, covering their mouths. "Oh! This is bad."

"Well?"

Alban looked at Gage and Gage scratched his head.

"Never mind," she said. "Just so we're clear on this one thing, neither of you may keep me."

"Then what can we do with you?" the boys asked.

"If, over time, you like me and I like you, we shall set out to become the best of friends."

To mark this rather unexpected occasion, the boys declared that something must be found for their new book. "But what shall it be?" they wondered, as they poked around in snake holes and birds' nests and mud in search of that right thing. Finally, it was decided. Along with a drip of blood and a drip of dew, they glued a Wingwee bathtub under the poem that appeared on Page One:

Skippily skip
A stone and a stick
A marble, a sunrise, a fly
Keep treasures close
That matter the most
And let all the rest skip by.

Gage and Alban were the children of two modern-thinkers and, as such, they did what they wanted when they wanted. Their mother was a poet known by one name: Cicely. Even to them, she was Cicely. Their father was Henry Livingstone Turnbull. *The* Henry Livingstone Turnbull. Suffice to say, had their parents been normal parents, the boys should not have been allowed to read his work for another ten years. While Cicely and Henry paced the widow's walk, smoking and looking to the treetops for inspiration, the two boys lost themselves in the garden without ever being missed.

This sort of freedom sounds magnificent if you're a little boy, but, sooner or later, it will lead to broken bones or something much worse. In Daisy Chain Garden, there were a series of stepping stones shaped by God to look like daisies, hence the name. If Cicely and Henry's parenting ideology were a daisy-shaped stepping stone, it would be the first in a series leading to disaster.

Petaloo, whose own parents had long since flown off to some other garden, took to meeting the boys each morning in the vesper flowers. The dark tunnels of their nostrils and their door-sized ears were as astonishing to her as her small acorn head was to them. She was exactly the same height as Gage Turnbull's tip-less finger and just about as slender. Whenever she stood by this woe-begone stump of a digit, an amazing thing happened. Her hair was no longer feltwort green but rather a fingery hue. It went the same when she sat in a buttercup or hopped onto a freckled dapperling mushroom. Like a chameleon, her hair turned buttercup yellow or freckly brown, blending in quite decoratively. Puddles did wonders for her eyes.

As for the brothers, she was not about to let them wander about with any regular old hair either. Of Gage, she said his hair reminded her of the sable paintbrush a monk once dropped in the honey fungus while passing through the garden. "I use it to tickle my face," she said. She flew on top of his head as she spoke, and tickled her nose with a bristle.

"And me?" Alban said. "What about my hair?"

Leaping onto the bent petal of a ragged robin, she thoughtfully considered Alban's locks. "Well, you're altogether different, aren't you, Fidget?" She called Alban *Fidget* sometimes. "You're not tickly at all. More like the pale wood of the spool I like to have my mint tea on."

"A spool!" he spat, not thinking a homely spool to be nearly as good as sable.

"*And* you have lily pad eyes," she was quick to add, for he was pulling such a face just then. "I long to leap just looking at them."

"Leap?" he snarled. "Where?"

"Why, right onto your *Shoe Upon* so you can take me on adventures."

This, you see, was what Petaloo did to Alban and Gage. She spun the hours away for them, making mountains of their mole hills and changing colors on a whim. The next keepsake they stuck in their book was a single braid of hair with three different ribbons of color: paintbrush, spool, and, *bruool,* a woody/ticklish chameleon-like combination that made for a shade all of its own. Petaloo so completely took over their days, nary a game of *Mipply Pipply* was remembered to be played.

But maybe you still have doubts as to the reality of such things? Think back. If you were lucky enough to grow up with a sibling, perhaps you can remember some small joy you shared with no one else but them? Something too crazy to be explained unless you had been there from the start. Maybe you had a Petaloo too, and you've simply forgotten after all these years? People do that, you know. The early beauty of a thing will be destroyed and squeezed to the back of a person's mind, if things take a turn for the worse later on. That doesn't make the Wingwees of childhood any less real. To the Turnbull brothers, Petaloo was real as rain.

Useful, too. A winged girl can be wonderful at pointing out where to dig for bones and other dead things. Six pages of rotten stuff came to be collected that first summer alone. Cicely forbid them to keep the book downstairs, that's how good it was. Petaloo had spent thousands of birthdays in Daisy Chain, so she could make her way around blindfolded and not stumble over a single pea.

"Thousands?" Alban said when she first revealed this to them. "How old are you anyway?"

"Four thousand and three and today is my birthday."

"But you look so young," Gage said.

"Oh heavens, no. Tomorrow, I'll be four thousand and four."

At that precise moment, Gage was carving a wine cork to make a boat. They intended to put Petaloo in the thing at Beatbones Rapid and watch her shoot the current. He blew a piece of cork fluff off the tip of his whittler. "You mean you have a birthday every day?"

"How else is a girl to celebrate life?"

Alban crossed his arms, feeling instantly cheated. "We do it once a year."

"Once a year? That's not nearly enough."

"We got bicycles last year. Do you get gifts on every birthday?"

"It wouldn't be a birthday without them."

"And cake?" Gage asked, scooping out a little seat.

"Are you mad?" she said. "Of course there's cake!"

Alban was standing knee-deep in the stream. He was to be the launcher. "Who gives you these presents?"

"Hopefully you. Every day, I show up with a jewel or a cat leg or a treasure map, but have I ever gotten so much as a *Happy Birthday* from you?"

"We didn't know," Gage said, jiggling his pockets. Most of her gifts ended up in the leather book, but some were too queerly shaped. He kept these in his pockets. Pen nubs, walnuts, shoe buckles...He made quite a racket when he walked. His favorite was the peach stone that looked like a bright red heart. Alban had insisted it might be secured in the book as easy as an abalone button, but, of course, it bent the pages and prevented the book from closing. Gage had taken to sleeping with it under his pillow and touching it in the dark.

Why would he touch an old seed in the dark, you might ask?

It was just some dumb peach stone, or so that's what Alban said after it refused to lie neatly in the book. But Alban had forgotten what Petaloo told them when she first rolled it onto his foot. "It's a Clingstone."

"What's it for?"

"For clinging, silly."

Sometimes, Gage was terrified that Petaloo would change gardens like her parents did. Touching the Clingstone made him feel better.

"I have five quid," Alban announced on the day of Petaloo's four thousand and third birthday. "What shall I buy you?"

Petaloo had never bought anything, though she'd read about it in the adverts that tumbled by from time to time. Alban explained about *Hibbert's Tools and Fine Sewing Goods* and Petaloo decided it might be nice to have a Fine Sewing Good. All thoughts of launching her were dropped at this point. Alban sprinted off, promising something remarkable.

Gage wrapped his fingers around the peach stone, tracing the ridges with his fingernail. If Alban bought something from *Hibbert's*, what sort of present might he give? Not the cork boat, surely. Petaloo had only agreed to the cork boat in order to shut them up.

After much consternation, Alban gave Petaloo a lace ribbon and Gage gave her a little chair. The ribbon cost half what Alban had in his mason jar and made Petaloo shriek like a jackdaw. Gage knotted together hedge mustard to make the chair, the first of a hundred pieces of furniture he would build for her. She sat in it all afternoon.

There was cake too. Alban whipped up some frosting and spread it on an orange jellybean. Petaloo had never had frosting before. Smacking her lips, she declared it her new favorite thing, never suspecting that something so sweet would one day spell doom.

After the boys made the decision to have birthdays every day too, they aged very quickly. They shouldn't have been surprised to wake up with moustaches or find grey in their sable, their lives were zipping so. In fact, if birthdays were stepping stones, they would be the next stone in the path. Without really meaning to do it, Petaloo grew them up fast.

Instead of watching her bob past cattails on a cork, the Turnbulls became locked in a competition to decide who was the most generous. Their treasures changed, too. No longer did they care about the shoehorn waiting to be unearthed by the garden gate.

"Here is the leftover twine from the rocker *I* made for Petaloo," Gage might say, placing twine in the book where otherwise a nice spore of witch's butter might have been glued instead.

"And here is the receipt for the thimble *I* bought off the *High-Priced Items* shelf." Alban would brag, covering up the twine. Page Ten is a puzzle of left-over handiwork and price tags slapped in place around this very poem:

> *Dimily dim*
> *By plot or by whim*
> *A memory will oft lose its way*
> *When one makes you grin*
> *Pray, store it within*
> *And you'll grin yet another day.*

Sadly, the boys weren't grinning much, and if you take a magnifying glass to Page Ten, you might be able to pick out the faintly purplish, lightly lemon-scented tear of a Wingwee left to dry on a receipt for a ruby button.

Sharing one finger-high girl between them was growing more and more difficult. If Petaloo should sometimes prefer Alban's high jinks to Gage's dark, quiet ways, favorite toys would be stomped to bits. A head might be held under water, even. Similarly, if Petaloo dared to admire Gage's ability to turn bedstraw into a working chest of drawers, miniature dining room sets would be sent flying. Petaloo began to prefer when the boys visited alone. There was peace then... for the most part.

When Alban came without Gage, great fun was sure to be had. He would sit her on the soft pink cushion of his palm and run like the devil, her long hair streaming between his fingers. Once, he tied her on his kite and flew her up to the sky. Another time, he fastened her to his shoestring and leapt off Hollar Rock. In these carefree moments, when the trees all blurred and warm skin made for the happiest of chariots, Alban was not competitive or cross or cruel. He was just Alban, falling breathless on his back in the flowers with his beloved Petaloo tumbling to rest on his stomach.

"Someday I'm going to marry you," he promised her on one such glorious day.

Settling her bottom on the circle of his shirt button, Petaloo asked, "Could we have a cake made out of frosting?" Not long before this, she had found a napkin with a picture of a wedding cake on it and had made it her parlor rug. Petaloo thought wedding cakes to be one of the finest of all human creations.

Alban raised up on his elbows and bright purple stamens bowed and parted around the shape of him. "Do you love me, then?"

"I couldn't darn your socks, I shouldn't think, nor hang your washed clothes up to dry on a line. For that matter, I couldn't wash them to begin with."

"Hm," Alban said. "I shouldn't like to do all that for myself. But what about love?"

"I don't believe in saying *that* word."

"Why not?"

"It's too powerful for Wingwee lips. It's too powerful for Boy lips, too."

"I won't always be a boy."

"Yes, but I will always be a Wingwee."

Alban had not considered this, as he was not normally given to consider anything overly much. "Come on," he said, scooping her up. "Let's jump off Crooked Bridge and scream until our lungs bleed."

On other days, a jingling jangling sort of romance bloomed, or so that's what it sounded like to Petaloo. With Gage, there was no screaming until you hurt yourself. No wayward kites. No proposals of marriage. On these more somber, clatter-pocket days, wood chips whizzed past Petaloo's head while she sunned herself on a geode and Gage built swings and canopy beds. He was taller now and stringy of limb. His hair hung in black, pointy quills that hid his eyes and there was no need to nickname such a boy as this, for the name Gage suited his contemplative soul as fittingly as Fidget suited his brother. She was grateful he did not speak of love as Alban did, though she'd often watched him roll the Clingstone between his hands in a way that made *her* fidget.

His voice was deep and hoarse and sad. "I built a chair for my father today, but it looked an awful mess."

"I don't believe it," Petaloo said. "Your creations would be beautiful in any size."

"No. I'm used to thinking small now. Perhaps I could make furniture for doll houses some day?"

"It would be a grand day for dolls if you did."

He shrugged. "I wouldn't like it as much as I like making things for you."

"I could go to having human birthdays, if that would free you up a little?"

The wood whittles stopped flying. "What an awful idea. We mustn't change things in the least."

This was her dream as well. On every first star every night, Petaloo wished to stop time. "Give me your hand," she said. Every so often, she felt compelled to do a test and stand herself next to his second to last finger.

"You're shrinking!" Gage cried.

Tears, smaller than seed pearls, tumbled from her eyes. "No, I'm not. You're growing. It's what you humans do best."

He rubbed his finger against her head and, for a split second, it seemed like seed pearls might fall out of his eyes, too. Then he thrust her back on the rock and took up his work once again, but not before he gripped the Clingstone and gave it a hard squeeze.

After a thousand birthdays, a new game came to be played between the brothers. It was called *Petaloo Who?* To play it, a boy was required to summon enormous indifference, if not all-out amnesia. It became the height of immaturity to admit to paying a visit to the garden. Much better, one should pretend to need some selfheal for a scratchy throat, if he was caught prowling around there.

Alban was better at this than Gage. If the name of Petaloo came up, Alban possessed the ability to look phenomenally confused, yet he still took a secret tramp through the garden daily to leave a crystal bead or a ball of yarn. Because self-preservation was at stake, the game of *Petaloo Who?* was infinitely more dangerous than *Nose Pins* would ever be.

One crisp, leaf-whirling afternoon, Alban stumbled into the garden with red-haired Edna Heat. Yes, *Heat*. It says so on her Baptismal certificate. Heat came to the garden and violets were rolled upon and brambleberries were squashed flat. Petaloo saw it all and even felt a bright green burst of something cold and hot explode inside her toothpick bones. It hurt so much, she limped for days after, certain Death was near. Despite confessing to her ineptitude with giant darning needles, she had foolishly imagined she could keep the boys forever in a cozy world of three. When Gage came clanking along hours later, she soaked his knee with her sobs, though she didn't tell him why. The poor boy was so distraught, he built her eight new sofas.

Blowing her nose on a pant's wrinkle, she looked up at him and knew beyond all shadow of a doubt that someday Gage would leave her, too. She climbed on his shoulder and rubbed her cheek against his, wishing, as she always did, to stop the hands of time.

But human nature is human nature, even if Wingwees refuse to cater to it. Party invitations replace saved candy wrappers on Pages Sixteen, Seventeen, and Eighteen in the book. And remember the kiss spit? Alban no longer dreamed of having a tiny wife. Miss Heat never flattened the brambleberries again, but a long list of others did. Alban had the sort of face every girl falls in love with. It would take a more special soul to pursue Gage.

Once, after both boys had stopped by on the sly — Gage before school and Alban after — Petaloo was watching a peppered moth soar past the garden when a triangle of paper came cart-wheeling through the dog rose to knock her on her head. Often such rude clobberings were the work of a mindless paper sack or a tobacco tin run amuck, but this particular piece of rubbish was so fresh-white, it begged closer inspection. Unfolding the triangle took Petaloo all of time. Fortunately, each new layer revealed something to keep her interest up.

The first corner opened to the salutation: *Good Morning, Young Mister Turnbull*. The next contained parts of four different sentences. And the next, tidbits of seven. The second triangle, for instance, looked like this:

...such a relief to hear you love me too...
...ever since and I can't seem to get you out of my mind.
...it is unseemly for a teacher to fall prey to...
...therefore I must ask for the strictest discretion.

In this way, the letter was read by Petaloo, the beginnings jigging and the endings jagging, until it reached its end.

Faithfully Yours,
P

By the time she got to 'P', Petaloo had the whole thing spread in the grass, but I suppose you get the picture. The triangle was a love letter dropped by one of the young Mister Turnbulls. But which one? Petaloo only knew that she was losing them faster than her heart could stand.

At the time of the triangle, Gage (in human years) was sixteen and Alban a year behind. Petaloo knew nothing of teachers and what was allowed or not allowed to pass between them, but she had learned that boys of a certain age forget how to share. She understood that the note was meant to be a secret so she carefully re-triangled the paper and put it under the old boot that Gage had given her for rainy days. Sooner or later, she was sure the owner would reveal himself and then she would return the note.

If a day should pass without a visit from Alban, she would say to herself, *A-hah! I knew it! Woman or girl, Alban charms them all. For certain, he is Young Mister Turnbull!* But then it would happen that Gage would be very late or very distracted, and she would think, *A-hah! So this is why Gage never brings girls to the garden!* Oh, it was highly frustrating, to say the least. Discovering the truth was like opening a triangle one corner at a time

Just when it seemed a proper hint might never come along, Petaloo discovered Alban picking through the goat willow anxiously looking for something.

A-hah!

"What are you doing?" Petaloo asked, making him jump when she flew up behind.

"I'm going to make a sling shot so I can shoot Neville

Pipping after school tomorrow."

A likely story, the Wingwee thought, but she graciously offered to help find a forked stick. "What is school like?" Petaloo asked. "Do you and Gage have the same teacher?"

"School is boring. We have Miss Wilton."

Petaloo checked a nutlet for projectile potential. "Is she nice?"

"Fairly, but everyone likes our religion teacher best. We're learning about heathens."

"What's her name, then?"

Holding up a rather promising Y, Alban extended his arm and pulled back on an imaginary strip of rubber. "Mr. Seaton," he said. "But everyone calls him Peter."

Somehow, Petaloo had come to be the guardian of a secret so heavy that, although it was made of paper, she couldn't budge it from its hiding place no matter how hard she tried. She wondered why humans liked to keep such bulky things. By her experience, they took up far too much room, leaving you to get soaked in the rain.

When asked about Mr. Seaton, Gage agreed that he was the favorite one. And Miss Wilton's first name? Nobody knew. "Peter is more like a friend than a teacher," Gage said of Mr. Seaton.

The next day, Petaloo was startled when two sets of feet nearly trampled her flat. She had not heard them coming yet there they were, Gage's gigantic hobnail boots, alongside a scuffed pair of spectators. A man laughed and before you could say MIND YOUR STEP, a berry bucket came crashing down, caging her in darkness. Muffled talking and laughing followed.

Nothing makes one feel smaller than being trapped

under a berry bucket at a moment such as this. You can imagine then how well Petaloo took it when Gage at last lifted the lid and, dumb as you please, said, "How did you get under there?"

"As if you don't know!"

"I must have kicked it without realizing," he said. *Kicked it without realizing!* She stormed off into the catmint and hid there until after he went home.

That night, she noticed Gage had left the leather book behind with a new footstool sitting on top of it. *I'm Sorry, Petaloo,* he'd written on a scrap pale blue paper. *I brought the book so we could look at it, but I couldn't find you anywhere. Perhaps tomorrow?*

Petaloo tried out the new footstool. It was the nicest one yet. She thought of the forlorn sound his pockets made when he'd given up and left. For a girl used to having her baths in a leaf, privacy was hard to understand. Much as it hurt her to think of it, Gage was old enough to deserve his privacy. Any day now, he would empty his pockets and move on. Petaloo wasn't sure she could bear to see the peach pit heart discarded in the weeds.

All night she lay awake, praying for young children to take the place of her two grown boys. The wishing star came and went in the sky. After serious thought, Petaloo arrived at a decision. Tomorrow would be her last birthday in Daisy Chain Garden. The time had come to move on. She worked a long time to open the book, and, with a sniff, placed Gage's note between the pages for him.

Now then, it seems we've come to the *frosting* part of the story. As hinted at all those words ago when bird skeletons were still the height of good fun, this next part you'll not like to hear. Even so, all books need an ending and the leather one is filled up now — all but one final page.

Let's turn to it.

Gage arrived the next morning, bearing a special present. "It's real wedding cake," he told her. "Can you find it in your heart to forgive me?"

"I've already forgiven you."

"And the book?" he said. "Can we read the book?"

She smiled, thinking how relieved he'd be to get his love note back. He carried her down to Beatbones Rapid to eat cake and flip through the book with her. "Here it is," Gage said. "The best page of all." He opened to that old tub.

It was shriveled now but, thanks to the blood, you could still see its faint shape. "Remember the first time we saw you? I thought you were a beetle."

"I'll never forget it, book or no."

"Me either."

"What's this?" he said, tapping his finger on a yellow-brown stain beside a shiny wing. "Who saved this?"

Petaloo felt so content, she only saw the wing. "Can we have some cake now, Gage?"

Get ready, because here it comes...

"Yes."

Quiet as that, Alban appeared, and what do you think he saw? Petaloo licking a fluffy swirl of white frosting off his brother's tip-less finger. "My favorite," said the girl, licking Gage's crooked finger until it was clean.

"Alban?" Gage said, looking up from her tongue. "Why are you wearing my boots?"

Alban squinted at them both. "I always wear yours in the garden. I don't like to get mine dirty."

Gage squinted too. "But they're *my* boots."

"At least I'm not sneaky like you, meeting by the rapids with wedding cake."

"You don't like to play in the garden anymore, remember?"

But Petaloo, for the first time, understood that this was not entirely true.

"You're a rat!" Alban sneered. Gage put down Petaloo with the book and jumped to his feet. As a fight broke out between the two, Petaloo, quick as her size would allow, began flipping the keepsake-heavy pages in search of the note. It was Fidget's triangle, she realized now. It was not for Gage to see.

"Let go," Gage said as Alban's hands plunged into his brother's pockets and began to tear through them.

"This junk belongs to me, too." Hateful words were shouted then, and fists were heard crunching jaws. Something red flew through the air. Blood, you might guess, but no.

While the Clingstone catapulted overhead, Petaloo turned to the note resting atop this last poem:

Sweepity Sweep
All that is cheap
For the years are quick to depart.
Keepity Keep.
The things that run deep
Save your best treasures inside your heart.

Then...*shhhplunk.*

Gage heard the seed hit the water and Alban spotted the note. With that, the hand of time, caught in its spiteful cog. Nothing breathed. Nothing bled. Nothing sunk.

Alas, time will have its own stubborn way in the end and it kicked and pushed until it got things rolling again. To compensate for the mix-up, it moved faster than ever.

Gage jumped toward the current, set on rescuing that old pit. Alban, just a step behind, thought Gage was going for the note, and jumped toward the book. Petaloo thought Gage wanted the letter too, and leapt up on the page to push the note into the stream. You might think her incapable of handling something so big with any amount of real speed.

Sometimes, the littlest thing will surprise you.

She scooted the triangle across the page as both boys drew closer. Alban's shadow reached her the same second she sent the note into the water. But his hand was already in motion, striving to hide something that was no longer inside the book — his actions too swift to take into account what was. In other words, he didn't see the Wingwee. He only saw his secret. And Gage, in turn, saw only that old stone.

In the tick of that epochal second, the Clingstone was snatched up, the note bobbed off in the current, and a wall of paper rose toward Petaloo, the words on the page growing larger and larger, before darkness came...

Keepity Keepity Keep.

The Blue Word

At Salvation House, you had to be an upper classman to play Leaves of Destiny. I don't know who made up that rule, but we were very strict about it. If you were in Grade Two or Grade Six or Grade Eleven and could be trusted not to squirm, you could sit in a folding chair and watch. The girls, I'm proud to say, were better at this than the boys.

Leaves of Destiny had ancient roots that were entirely non-Catholic, yet the sisters permitted it like they permitted Buck Buck or Bilboquet. They pretended not to spy as the Grade Twelvers cloaked themselves in white and passed around the Bible every year on the first night in November. Their whispers behind the curtain were as much a tradition as any other part of the game.

I watched, holding my breath every year, looking forward to my own turn more than I looked forward to anything else in my life. When it finally came, God sent a shower of ice that turned the trees beyond our windows into a forest of broken glass. Perhaps it was a warning.

Eyes shut, I held the book on the upturned palm of my left hand (as is the official way) and prepared to pick a place with my right. Thousands of other destinies whispered by in a flutter of tissue pages. My finger sought the one that was meant to be my own. "Here," I said, stabbing blindly and picking out a verse.

The girl to my left had just chosen something lovely from Exodus about sashes and headbands, and the girl before her had fingered *four cups made like almond blossoms*. The almond blossoms made everyone gasp. I had every hope that my own choice would be something equally special.

A sharp limb tapped at the window just then, chasing the flower cups from my head. I opened my eyes, ready to behold my future.

Dead flies cause the oil of the perfumer to send forth an evil odor; so does a little folly outweigh wisdom and honor.

Even the nuns laughed. It turns out I'd waited all this time for folly and dead flies.

After the game, I couldn't help but feel anxious when confronted with foul smells. I was on the lookout for flies everyplace I went. Two weeks before graduation, the rank whiff of destiny found me at long last.

We were asleep when the first projectile came crashing through our burning roof. I thought it was a boulder at first, until it splattered against the linen cupboard in a firework of red droplets. More fireworks followed. The monsters were catapulting things at us from outside the school walls.

"Looks like pork," my best friend, Corinthians, said. She squatted by the mess and gave it a closer look.

Meat might sound like odd ammunition, but we were used to variety. Never mind that there was no shortage of proper stones to sling, the monsters seemed to favor more indignant things. We once got hit with some running shoes, which came in handy afterwards. Another time, they threw doll heads. I only cared that the ammo this time was sure to leave blood stains.

Burning bits of ceiling rained down with the meat. Someone's head caught fire. Before poor Deuteronomy could let out a scream, the bells started playing *Jesus Wants me for a Sunbeam* and Sister Sabastienne ran into the room. "Safety Positions, children!"

I was the one to smother Deut's blackened skull, though she never thanked me for it. "Damn you, Esther!" is what she said after I finished smacking her with the pillow. The room was filling with smoke and pork, so there was no time to bother about that.

"Buckets," Sister said.

Usually, the bells signaled a drill. Every so often, the alarm meant something more. I'd been Second Girl on the brigade since I could stand on two feet. We formed a snake down St. Jhudiel's Hall, passing water to Sister Edwige on her ladder.

"They've broken through the keep," Sister Edwige reported, for she could see the monsters from her perch and was never one for shielding us from the truth, like some of the others. "One of the guards is down!"

Salvation House was located inside the walls of Castle Montségur on a cliff in the Pyrenees. Before chalk boards and desks were added, people used to pay for historical tours. Archaeologists once searched the site for a manuscript called the *Book of Love* that had been hidden in the castle years before. The book was made of palm leaves soaked in peacock blood and was said to contain revelations confided by our Lord Jesus Christ, the words of which were so powerful, they need only be heard, and all hatred, anger, and jealousy would vanish from the heart of man. Anyone who touched the book would be attracted to the leaves of their destiny within, hence our little game. We'd spent many an hour poking about dark cervices looking for the thing without any luck. Fortunately, a regular Bible worked much the same as substituting a five franc coin will replace a missing tidly-wink.

Jesus' most consequential words were not the only feather in Montségur's cap. A stele by the Pepsi machine marked the spot where a group of religious zealots had been killed in a bonfire centuries before:

> In This Place On 16th March 1244
> More Than Two Hundred People Were Burned.
> They Chose Not To Abjure Their Faith.

Most of what I knew about the zealots came from teenagers hoping to scare little kids. It wasn't all made-up stuff, though. The Junior Wing sometimes smelled of smoke, even when we weren't being pelted with flaming arrows. There's a cry people make when their skin is blistering off their bones. I shouldn't have known what that sounded like, but I did. I'd heard it many a night. Sister Sabastienne said it was just the wind because she wanted us to smile all the time. But everyone knows that wind does not whimper as though its tongue is being boiled in the bowl of a dying mouth.

After The Devastation, guard towers were built around the keep. The Routiers attacked anyway.

'Routier' was the nice name the sisters used for those who lived beyond the walls. Corinthians saw them once when she was helping paint the belfry. She said the creatures were hideous, their arms as thick as bread loaves and their cheeks badly bloated. I asked her what their skin was like because we'd all heard so many rumors. Some of them were puffy and pink, she said. Some were puffy brown. Their skulls were covered with thick wild hair and they moved in snarling droves.

Even though our student population was composed of orphans, only the best and brightest were allowed to live at Salvation House. The monsters did not like us because of this. We had bars on the windows and locks on all the doors. They were more vicious than ever the night of the attack. As if smelly meat was not quite insulting enough, a fiery arrow hit Sister Sabastienne in the shoulder.

"Be strong children," she told us as she went down. "Remember who you are!"

"The Blessed," we answered in one clear voice, saying it like you say "Amen". We said these same words every day. Sometimes Deuteronomy mumbled them in her sleep.

Being The Blessed was not something to be vain about, but the sisters said it was important to remember how fortunate we were, especially in these difficult times. The countryside was full of heathens who thrived on violence. They lived without the hope of finding a *Book of Love*. There were precious few who had any destiny at all. Instead of God, the Infected worshipped flesh, craving it like air. I'd heard a thousand history lectures, but I would not be seeing things for myself until my Leaving Ceremony.

"Must protect the children," Philemon said, stepping over Sister Sabastienne and swinging his protection stick. With his shadowy eyes and smooth, pale skin, Philemon was the most beautiful of the beautiful. Given the high standards at our school, this was no small thing. He hurled his stick through the hole in the roof and let loose a warrior cry. Later, he would be bawled out for losing his stick, but that lone act seemed magnificent to us. Salvation House was a hive of self-preservation. Although the guards would shoot Routiers if forced, the rest of us spent every attack the same way — dutifully keeping ahead of the flames. There was no thought of fighting back. Until this night.

To see Sister Sabastienne bleeding on our hand-embroidered *Let the Children Come to Me* rug was more than we could bear. Had we all been holding our sticks instead of buckets, we'd have let loose a shower of spears on the backs of those ugly monsters and brought them to their knees! Salvation House had taught us to love, yet a dark finger of hatred began to poke around inside of me.

For a minute, I forgot the biggest rule of all: *A grateful child counts her blessings and remembers to keep the peace.* In two weeks, my class would be entering the out-world for the first time ever. Usually, this thought delighted me beyond description. Now I experienced something terrible in my soul. I thought it might be *terror,* but I couldn't be sure.

Oh, I'd sat up many a night with a pumping heart, listening to ghosts choking in the throes of burning death, but fear, for the most part, was not allowed. At Salvation House, no one was afraid of the dark because there were nightlights everywhere. The same could be said for crawling things. Spiders were stamped out the minute they were spotted, so there was no need to get hysterical. Thunderstorms were angel burps, and lockers took up the space under a bed where otherwise vile beasties might have lain in wait. If only the sisters could have gotten their hands on them, the ghosts would have found themselves flushed down the pipes with the rest of the scary stuff, I'm certain of it. Even Routiers normally caused no more damage than a missed hour of math.

Now, I was shaking at the thought of living among these monsters with no guard towers in between us. That hateful finger of fear ran up the stalks of my organs to wedge securely in my throat. We'd all seen the charts in first hour World Preparation. Small tribes of the diseased still roamed the nether-reaches of almost every country, their symptoms temporarily suppressed by illegal doses of Lariathol.

"But don't despair, children," Sister Edwige told us. "Elimination rates are up ten percent this year."

As I wiggled my house slipper out from underneath an exploded ham butt, I tried to look on the bright side. I imagined the private room I would live in at Job Corp while receiving my training. I had such high hopes for the place. In fact, I'd colored in three boxes on the Placement Form even though it said to pick only one: DOCTOR. WIFE. MOTHER. At the time, Sister Sabastienne praised me for having such big dreams.

After I worked my slipper loose, I hid my face in my hands and cried. I could tell the meat was never going to wash out of the fluff.

Once the danger was over, Sister Sabastienne was carried off to hospital and I was given nursing duty. Corinthians got clean-up. While she swept and scrubbed and tossed out burnt pillows, I patted a cool rag on Deut's sore head and tried not to listen as Sister Sabastienne's arrow was being yanked out. A couple of people slipped in her blood, so this gave me more patients to look after. I still heard too much.

Sister Arnaude, who ran the ward, and Father Barthelemy, who ran the school, stood around in the blood, debating whether to send out for help or not. In the end, they decided to patch up Sister Sabastienne and give her lots of medicine. Not the little red *Keep Well* pills we all took in order to stay disease-free. This medicine looked like water and it went into her arm through a fat needle. The water-medicine was to stop the pain.

"Does it really hurt so bad that she needs a needle stuck inside her?" I asked Sister Arnaude.

Before she could answer, Sister Sabastienne jerked fitfully and spoke for the first time since they'd pulled her arrow out. "Hurts like a son of a bitch," she said.

That's how I found out that the water-medicine made Sister Sabastienne willing to answer any question, even if the answer wasn't something that would put a smile on your face.

◯

The way the sisters taught The Great Devastation was enough to put you to sleep for good. Somehow, it didn't feel that important.

What year did Strasbourg fall? What ecological crisis is blamed for starting the outbreak? How many people died worldwide?

It was just a lot of numbers and old stuff that happened a long time ago. We couldn't fathom what had been lost because we'd never seen the world as it once was, or what had been left in its place. Only one part appeared to apply to us:

In order to preserve the innocent lives of those orphaned due to the Great Devastation, sister Nathalie Maryse negotiated with new world government to set up a safe haven for the blah blah blah blah blah...

I was in my last semester of Honor and Duty after twelve long grueling years. I'd spent two years in Brotherly Concepts and a year in Out-World Ethics. It was only in the last hour, I'd managed to muster a proper interest in the events of the past. Still, I might never have begun the secret interrogations, had Corinthians not shown me the rock.

She came across it while mopping our room. One of the Routiers had thrown a stone with four words written on it in blue paint and it ended up under Corinthian's bed. "What do you think it means?" she asked me.

"I think we should ask Philemon," I said.

Philemon could finish a book in less than a month and

he had a very talented tongue. He could say *six thick thistle sticks* as fast as you please without getting twisted up at all. When we gave him the rock, he tapped his finger on the words as if he could wake up the letters and make them explain themselves.

"*Humbies?*" he said. "Never heard of it."

That afternoon, I was pouring tea for Sister Sabastienne when she began to twitch. "Back, you miserable demons!" she shouted.

Hmm, I thought.

"Is it the Humbies, Sister?" I asked, taking hold of her hand.

I recalled the noises I'd heard during the attack. The mush-mouthed fury of the monsters was a language I could not understand.

"Don't call them that," Sister said when she heard me say the blue word. "It isn't right to say such cruel things. They're God's creatures, too. Don't call them by that *name*."

"What should I call them then?" I asked.

Her tongue punched against her sealed lips, but it did not break free.

"Say it!" I urged. "What should I call them?"

Two words rushed out with the force of a cough. "The Blessed," Sister Sabastienne said.

I pictured the painted words in my head: *Death To All Humbies*.

"Well?" Corinthians asked me later. "Does Sister Sabastienne know what Humbies are?"

"Yes."

"And?" she said as she clapped her hands excitedly, certain it would be something fun.

"Humbies are *us*."

They let me sit up that night and keep an eye on things because Sister Sabastienne was so restless. I was to call first thing if there was trouble. I used the opportunity to ask more questions.

"Why do the monsters call us Humbies?" I asked. I thought she was still delirious like before, but she opened her eyes and looked at me, very surprised.

"Where did you hear that word, Esther Six?"

I knew she was upset because she used my full name. Unlike Sister Edwige, who always just called me Six, Sister Sabastienne only used our last names when she was really worked up about something.

I showed her the rock.

"Oh dear. How many children have seen this?"

"Plenty," I told her, and it wasn't really a fib. "Everyone is demanding to know what it means."

Sister waved the idea away. "Routiers never speak sense. It doesn't mean anything."

Hearing her lie shocked me terribly and hurt my heart in the most shivery of places. I left the ward with the intention of taking a nap, but I knew I wouldn't be able to sleep. I hadn't slept in weeks. Before the attack, my sleeplessness was due to excitement. For as long as I could remember, I'd raced to the departure platform every graduation day to watch the graduates enter the Leaving Car and descend to their new lives. It was important to get there early for a good spot so you could get a last look as the glass elevator bore them away: first feet, then shoulders, then smiles...Rumor had it, there was a champagne toast waiting at the bottom, but that was a private affair. For the rest of us, the Leaving Car was the end of it.

Oh, the graduates still visited us, but only in memories. The yellow wall that led to the platform was plastered with snapshots of their faces. There was

Genesis Twelve from a few years back, her picture slightly crooked. Genesis had been voted "Class Clown" and in her picture, the blue ties of her uniform were tied in front instead of in back. Lips puckered, she was blowing a giant bubble that painted her face every color of the rainbow. My old friend Proverbs was in the photo next to Gen's. Proverbs had been frozen in time jumping across the finish line in a sack race. The shriek she'd shrieked when she hopped to victory was so loud, it was still echoing around our school a year later. I was especially fond of the photo of the first Mark One, though I'd never met the boy. Before Philemon got handsome, I'd planned to look him up in the out-world and see if he wanted to get married. He was juggling little red balls in his photo and I thought he might be willing to teach me how to do this after we became friends. I'd fallen into the habit of patting his picture every year, as if to say, "See you soon." Corinthians reminded me that the first Mark One would be an old man now.

This year it was going to be *our* year. Soon, our pictures would be joining the others on the wall. It would be our turn to step into the car. Maybe one of the younger students would pat my picture when they passed by? Just thinking about the big day had made me dizzy with longing.

But that had changed.

I tried to sleep, but I kept hearing a buzzing in my ear. Flies circled as though I were a hunk of meat. Before I knew it, the wrinkles in my blanket had all transformed into bread loaf-sized arms reaching out for me. Moaning Routiers stalked the twisty tunnels of my mind, their breath reeking of rot. *Death To All Humbies*. When sleep finally came, it took me in spasms.

Ten minutes later, I was jarred awake by the sickly dings of *Jesus Wants me for a Sunbeam*. Everyone else was in the Honor assembly and got to see it, first-hand, when the bullet chipped the chapel window. Me, I covered my head with my pillow and waited for a flaming arrow to strike me someplace bad.

The blue word soured everything, turning my last days at Salvation House into a nightmare. Instead of wrinkling my nose at the Wednesday menu and thanking God that I would soon be free to eat what I liked, I felt tears prickle at the back of my eyes as if the potent stench of liver sorbet was the perfume of my long-lost mother. One afternoon, while grumbling about the shower line that wrapped from here to there and back again, it hit me like a lightning bolt that this was the very place where my friends and I always laughed the hardest. And who would sleep in Bed 45 after I was gone? I began to worry about this non-stop.

I hoped it would be someone who would hang her class ribbons from the grill and keep her shower cap on the post. I hoped, too, that she would leave Philemon's name on the wood where I'd painstakingly chiseled it with a paperclip. I'd not sanded off the things I'd found there. There was still a reminder to leave a candle burning on the windowsill in case the Virgin Mary passed by, and I'd long ago made my peace with the words *Your Feet Smell*, that someone had taken more time with than I had taken with my true love's name. The plastic pearls of a stranger were knotted around one leg. I'd kept those, too. I hoped whoever came after me was clever enough to store secret things in the little dip under the mattress. Not every mattress had one.

I was going to miss Bed 45. I blamed this on the blue word.

After the pork bombs, Salvation House suffered from a fly infestation that proved tormenting for all. I was worried about my destiny, of course. Others routinely mistook the flies for mosquitoes. Sister Arnaude proved particularly squeamish. Father had sprayed the ward ten times but the flies kept re-appearing. One morning, a fly walked across her cheek, and she jumped around, flapping her arms and swatting angrily. Because Father was saying mass at the time, she put a key in my hand and said, "Fetch me the bug traps."

I'd been inside Father's office a few years earlier when Corinthians and I were playing angels in the *le Réveillon* pageant. Sister Edwige had stopped off for masking tape to fix my torn wing and I took in as much as I could, hoping to see something that spoke of a secret, and I did. There were filing cabinets with keyholes under every drawer handle. There was an envelope next to the masking tape marked *security code*. There was a phone with a red button labeled *private line*. I lived a life without any keyholes, so I'd found this very mysterious. When we were leaving with the tape, Sister Arnaude bumped a shelf that had a plate collection on it. The plates had belonged to Father Barthelemy's mother and a couple of them broke. While we were cleaning up, I pocketed a piece of china with Bertha of Burgandy's head on it. It was going to be thrown out anyway. I hid the head in my mattress dip.

When Sister Arnaude gave me the office key, it was like a lit firecracker inside my fist, but I acted nonchalant when I used it on the lock. My face said, "I'm here on official bug business."

Pretending not to see the tremendous stock of traps in the corner, I started to search. There was a book on the desk with a sticky note on it. *Choose Photos*. I recognized the book at once. The sisters had been pasting pictures in it since the doors opened on Salvation House. I was in the book wearing a taped wing.

Next, I found a newspaper clipping. At the top was a

photograph of a bride, but her fluffy veil made it hard to see her underneath. Someday I wanted to marry Philemon and wear a fluffy veil just like the one in the picture. Philemon seemed agreeable.

The previous New Year's Eve, when I was getting more cups for the punch and Philemon was getting more ice from the freezer, we'd both stopped in the middle of the kitchen and looked at each other. Before I could think, he slid his hand through the tufts of my hair, daring to touch the bare places in between with his ice-cold fingers. No one had ever touched the skin on my head before, and I was sure we'd get detention, but it made me feel unspeakably happy and light. When Sister Sabastienne walked in, we were standing in a puddle of melting ice cubes.

Sister reminded me that I was to save such things for after graduation. Luckily, she let it go at that. I never forgot how nice it was though. I hoped to touch Philemon's head after we were married.

Under the bride was a recipe for something called *Tex-Mex Chili* and an article about our school:

Amid a fresh burst of public outcry, Salvation House releases a new report claiming to have saved the lives of over two hundred cross-bred children since The Devastation.

Hmm, I thought.

I finished reading the article in a bathroom stall, but the facts were all confused. The newspaper said that Salvation House was *a lock-down center for children of mixed heritage*. I was suspicious that the reporter was a jealous Routier:

Despite opposition, the government maintains that the need for such a facility is strong. The Minister of Health and Solidarity met with outraged citizens in Dunkerque this week to address concerns.

"Whether or not the law prohibits marriage between the

well and the infected, Hybrids continue to be born," Boulanger said Tuesday. "The question is: are we as a society prepared to kill innocent babies because of parents who disregard the law?"

The article spoke of a place called *Salvation Out-Reach* where mothers could receive prenatal care and make a fresh start by turning over their children to the proper authorities without fear of prosecution. *While military forces seek to eliminate the lingering threat, a small segment of those suffering from Greenhouse Malaria have managed to get their hands on illegal doses of Lariathol, making their condition harder to detect.* The article cautioned people to be responsible and ask for a complete medical examination before partnering with anyone. *But carelessness is not always the culprit. While authorities continue to warn about the selective pressure Greenhouse Malaria puts on the human genome, there are still those choosing to engage in relations with the infected.*

Meanwhile, a group calling themselves S.A.V.E. (Students Advocating Victim Elimination) has been responsible for numerous outbreaks of violence in the capital city since November. An unidentified spokesperson for the group announced plans to begin targeting Salvation House itself if lawmakers will not hear their plea. S.A.V.E. is demanding legislation that would put into place the same elimination protocols for cross-species that exists for the infected...

Opening a folded flap next to these words, I came face to face with a picture of one of the monsters. I nearly threw-up. It was all the more awful in that the creature was a freakish distortion of a person. The arms and legs were in the normal places but they looked huge, as if its skin was really thick and there were no bones to speak of. The face was puffed up with fat, like the sisters', and the eyes were slitty and mean. There was hair in unnatural places, too — under the nose, on its chin, all over its giant head. Worse still, the thing had not been de-teethed.

Corinthians never said anything about seeing teeth. The sisters all suffered survivor effects from The Devastation but, at least, they didn't have teeth. In the picture, the monster was wearing a shirt that said: *Abortion Is The Law.*

Abortion?

This black word proved just as strange as the blue one.

All told, I was two hours getting through the whole article and still couldn't wrap my brain around it. For me, it was like hearing someone claim that the grass was red instead of green, or that Christmas would not be coming in April, August, and December. The last part was the most troubling of all:

Salvation House prides itself on giving life to the innocent, offering Hybrids something that could not be safely offered otherwise: Eighteen years.

Everyone knows that honor is a citizen's foremost duty. Without it, there would be chaos. Disregard the rules, and you may as well be a Routier. When I showed the article to Sister Sabastienne, she reminded me that I had been trusted with a job and that I had not lived up to that trust. She put the clipping in her nightstand, fully expecting me to shut-up honorably, but it was too late for that.

The article spelled things out reasonably well, but I still had questions. "Why?"

Sister Sabastienne took a deep breath. "In a few days, you're going to graduate and you'll have all your answers then."

For Christmas one year, Philemon had given me a drawing he made of a hawk soaring past his window. *Someday* it said. Someday was almost here. That didn't stop my need to know.

"Why didn't you tell us we're part human and part...*zombie*?"

"Don't use that word, dear."

"Humbies."

She clapped her hand over my mouth. "You are *The Blessed*, do you hear me?"

I pushed her hand away. "Are we really brighter and more beautiful?"

"To us, you are."

"To you? To the fifteen nuns who live here and Father Barthelemy? But not the rest of the world?"

"This is why we don't keep newspapers."

"To deceive us?"

"To give you peace in a troubled world. There are different truths, Esther. You know as well as I do that there is great joy to be found in our special family. Why should this be any less true than what goes on out there?"

Sister had not been able to sit up for three days, but she sat up now. "I want you to understand something. We've taught you about duty and honor and the importance of considering others. Like all people, you've found these things to be tested in your life, but never more than now. Salvation House exists on shaky ground. There are a lot of people waiting for us to slip up so they can pull the plug. If ever there is an escape or some sort of a revolt, Salvation House is to be shut down permanently."

"An escape? That makes it sound like a dungeon."

"Not a dungeon. A sanctuary. It is in everyone's best interest that you live within these walls. We have revealed and concealed different parts of history for a reason. Everyone must be content."

"So, you withhold the facts to keep the peace?"

"We tell as much as we can. It was originally proposed

that we not teach anything about The Great Devastation but we wanted to prepare you for the Routiers. It is difficult to untangle ourselves completely from the out-world."

"And if I won't keep quiet?"

"Then you will kill Salvation House."

I bit my lip. I had one more question and it was a big one. "The newspaper said we get eighteen years, as if that's all there is."

I could see It in her eyes as clear as a crack in a marble. Pity.

"It can't be," I whispered. World Preparation had been preparing us for a truth that did not exist! "We don't leave, do we?"

Sister was biting on her fist now, tears pouring down her face. "Let it go, Esther."

"What happens?"

She didn't want to tell me. She wept and begged, but I was without honor now. "What happens to us after we step into the Leaving Car?"

She wiped her eyes with the back of her hand. "Heaven," she said.

The bargain had been struck long ago. The world could not afford a third species, a mixing of the mixed. When our years were up, they promised us a graduation party and put us in a car filled with gas.

Sister tried her best to put a cherry on it. "The average life expectancy in the out-world is sixteen to twenty years. Eighteen is a good long life. It's better than killing babies."

Babies.

I saw mine then, the one that cooed in my imagination. "But how can I go through with this, Sister?"

"Think of that champagne toast," she said. "Think of your dreams. You're feeling sorry for yourself right now and all that you will never have, but remember this: a lot of people out there never get a real Christmas or a warm bed or good health or love. Most of them never know the luxury of having any dreams at all."

I didn't know if honor was really about honor anymore or if it was just another protection device like the Bucket Brigade. For the first time, I pictured shimmying down the bell rope and making a run through a forest I'd only seen from afar. It wouldn't be easy. I'd have to try and survive in a world that I knew less about this week than I did the week before. But at least I would be free. Free to learn the truth and turn nineteen and have a baby if I still wanted one.

They would shut down Salvation House, of course, but the place was a lie anyway. I'd be doing everyone a favor by exposing the truth. And sure, the other children would die and the program would end, but they were all dead anyway. Corinthians, Philemon, Deut...all of them caught up in a dream that would never be.

But wait!

I could take them with me. Well, I could take Corinthians. I could take Philemon. I pictured us charging Father with our protection sticks and making him let us out. Who did they think we were, anyway? They couldn't keep us down with honor. Buy us off with Christmas! Why should I step into that elevator and let them silence me? It was a bonfire for the faithful all over again, a bonfire they had been slowly luring us into since the first minute we drew breath.

I began practicing different ways to tell Corinthians. *You remember Gen Twelve and the first Mark One? Well, both of them are dead...*

I found her in the craft room pouring honey on strips of yellow paper. She was making flypaper for our Leaving Ceremony. "No bugs allowed," she said. I'd never seen her looking so happy.

Terrific.

"Guess what?!" she said. "Don't tell anyone, but we really do get to have champagne for the toast. Sister Sabastienne said we could."

"I'll bet she did," I said. I was sad and furious and ready to scream. A big part of me still wanted to see what Corinthians saw when she thought of graduation. Instead, all I could see was running through the trees into a world that didn't want me, while the one that did went up in flames at my back.

But I had to tell her. There was something wrong when a lie was made to be more honorable than the truth.

"Ew!" Cornithians said, holding up the honey paper. "I've already caught a fly."

It wiggled and kicked, its little wings stuck in the sugary glue. She said, "'Dead flies cause the oil of the perfumer to send forth an evil odor; so does a little folly outweigh wisdom and honor'."

"You memorized it?" I said.

"Of course. It's your destiny."

"Listen to me, Corinthians, I learned more about that blue word on the rock you found..."

"Did you memorize mine?" she asked

The poor girl. All she cared about was a stupid destiny that was never going to be.

"Mine is nice," she said. "Their wings were joined one to another. They didn't turn when they went. They went everyone straight forward."

With that, my best friend Corinthians, whom I loved with all my heart, set aside the flypaper and with a contented smile, began to blow up balloons.

We lined up girl-boy in the yellow hall, everyone laughing about the new pictures that had been tacked up on the wall. Corinthians said her nose looked big, but I could tell she was thrilled. We were in a picture together, scooping handfuls of bonbons and Orangettes out of our shoes on Christmas day. It was a nice shot. A good memory.

We'd spent this morning putting our things in boxes with our names on them. I wondered if my new espadrilles and my *Best Speller* ribbon would end up as someone's hand-me-downs, or if they would be burnt up in the furnace. We put our protection sticks in the athletics closet to be passed on. I folded up the picture of the hawk and left it with Bertha of Burgandy's head in the mattress dip. I said goodbye to Bed 45.

The younger students started jumping up and down as the Leaving Car cranked to a stop. "This is it," Sister Edwige said.

I glanced at Sister Sabastienne, watching as she swished a fly off her nose and tried not to look at me. The day before, she'd taken me aside and promised it would be quick. All I had to do was step in the car and I wouldn't feel a thing.

"So...what will you do, Esther Six?"

"I don't know."

The door to the Leaving Car slid open and everyone smiled and piled in. It wasn't too late to have my say. At that moment, every eye in the school was on me.

I knew their faces, each and every one. I knew them because they were me. I knew they would follow us as far as they could, wildly waving when the doors slid shut.

The doors slid shut. Everyone waved wildly.

Closing my eyes, I reached for Corinthian's hand and thought about the champagne toast that waited for me at the other end.

Maxwell Treat's Museum of Torture for Young Girls and Boys

"If you turn the lever the wrong way, you'll hear a click and a pitchfork will swoop down and skewer your big fat head like a juicy meatball," Max said. He pointed to a La-Z-Boy recliner cordoned off with hot pink jump ropes in the back of the museum. "You'll hear a click if you turn the lever the right way too, only the buckle will snap open and you'll get to go free." He gave the plaid thing a loving pat. "Don't let the lumbar support fool you, son. This baby is pure Spanish Inquisition."

"Which way is the right way?" Hayden asked.

Max winked a wink that made him look more like a used car salesman than a fourteen year old year old kid. "Why don't you hop in and find out?"

That was two weeks ago.

Two weeks ago, Hayden Finch had no intention of putting Max's weird chair to the test, but things change. Sometimes a boy can't help but find himself with a pitchfork aimed at his big fat head and no way out but to make a choice.

Everything he cared about had disappeared in a flash of light at the railroad crossing at the bottom of the hill on Hermosa Avenue. Hayden used to get excited when he saw the red and white arm of the gate going down, even though his mother usually cussed and said that now, they were sure to be late. He used to lift his feet when they rode over the track. For luck.

When he thought about that same railroad crossing now (which he did some fifteen or twenty times a day), he wondered if his dad had looked at his mom to get her input on the matter. Did Mom stick up her thumb and say, "Go for it, Larry?" Or, did she shake her head no? Maybe Dad didn't look at her at all. Maybe instead of looking at Mom, he'd looked at the 8:15 barreling toward them and made the decision all by himself. Hayden wished he knew so he could decide who to blame.

In any case, after the railroad crossing, Hayden was sent to Bible, Iowa, to live on a turkey farm with his cousins in a house that smelled of stale Oreos, dirty socks and pee. He was told to sleep where he liked and handed a set of faded Power Ranger sheets that had little brown holes burned through all the Rangers' eyes, except the Black one. He was introduced to three boys with a hobby so peculiar that things could only lead to a rusted lever and a right or wrong click.

His first day in his new home began with a demonstration.

"A good guillotine dumps the head in the basket for you," Max said, pulling the release on his guillotine. The blade shot down and split a grapefruit in a spray of pink blood. A drip of juice hung off the tip of Max's nose. It quivered when he breathed. "Like to try it?" he asked, his drip quivering faster.

At fourteen, Max was the oldest and most obsessive of the brothers, but Merkle was no less inclined to split things open and, anyway, his name was Merkle. *Merk*, they called him. Or Merky. It was a family name. Merk was thirteen, like Hayden. The youngest was called Minor. Minor was taller than Merk. The brothers were building a torture museum in their garage. Hayden took one look at Maxwell's guillotine and cursed his parents as he had never cursed them before.

When they weren't tending turkeys, everyone had a job to do. Minor made signs that said things like: *Ten more miles to Iowa's most torturous torture museum* or *Last chance for torture — take exit 210 and turn right at McDonald's*. He tipped the signs so the red letters would run. Merkle was transforming the tomato patch into a parking lot. Max was in charge of the devices. Seeing how Hayden was the only torture novice in the group, he did duty with each of the brothers in order to learn the ropes.

"What's Uncle Tommy say about you having a guillotine?" Hayden asked after witnessing the grapefruit execution. "Isn't he worried you'll hurt yourself?"

"Naw. Daddy thinks tourism would be good for Bible. Would you believe it, there ain't a decent torture museum for a hundred miles around?"

Max was an enterprising boy. There was no disputing that. He'd set up a website asking people to donate their medieval torture devices to the cause. Hayden laughed at first, but the packages kept coming.

"Now, what is that one, dear?" Aunt Tawny would ask every time Max unveiled a new gadget.

"In-step borer, Ma."

The new in-step borer made Aunt Tawny giggle and bury her face in a dishtowel. "You be careful with that,

Maxwell."

The brothers wanted the place to be a family museum that offered something for everyone. They sketched their ideas in colored pencil and hung them up and down the fridge. A boy couldn't hardly get himself a Jell-O cup, there was such a landmine of magnets to be negotiated. If you knocked things out of order, you got punched.

The plans were meticulously detailed. In the lobby, families would be able to dress in rags, climb in the stocks, and get a Polaroid taken for three bucks. For five bucks, the Treats would jeer and bounce cabbages off your skull. There would be Hands-On exhibits for the little ones to enjoy: a tongue-curb, a finger-straightener, a Spanish Tickler. Minor had created educational Paint-by-Number sets for the bigger kids. Grown-ups would enjoy a pictorial history of the devices in action.

One day, Max suggested practicing his tour guide skills on Hayden, offering him *The Curious Boy's Special*, which included a Gatorade and a peek in the Off-Limits Room at the back of the museum. Max had printed his spiel on a set of green index cards, but he tried not to look at them when he talked.

"First up, we have something called Tucker's Telephone donated by Mr. Herman Long of Cotter, Arkansas. This phone might look like a plain old crank telephone, but it's been wired with two dry cell batteries and it will give you the shock of your life if you crank it. Tucker's Telephone was damaging organs as late as 1968 at the Tucker State Prison Farm." Max checked his cards. "Care to make a call, little miss?" he asked.

"On your right, we have a genuine certified replica of a Brazen Bull, brainchild of the Tyrant of Agrigentum himself. Prisoners were put in the brass belly and roasted alive. To keep the mood fun during executions, the ox head was designed with a system of tubes that converted the prisoners screams into sounds like those of a bellowing bull. As an added advantage, the victim's scorched bones shone like gems afterward, and could be made into lovely bracelets..."

Hayden sipped grape Gatorade as thumbscrews crushed the bones of Virginia slaves and 'Judas Chairs' reaped havoc on the bottoms of luckless Protestants. Max was a real showman, gesturing grandly and making pop-eyes at invisible patrons. "Last, but not least, we come to the Off-Limits Room. Now, girls and boys, this is a room that only very special individuals ever get to see."

"Yeah, those that cough up five bucks," Hayden laughed.

"Shhhh. You may think you've seen it all, folks, but I warn you, the devices in this room are far too horrid to be shown to the ordinary public. If anyone has second thoughts, I advise you to turn back now." Max paused. His eyes swept from one side of the garage to the other. "Anyone?" Another pause. "Very well. Enter at your own risk."

Some of the hinges in the museum had been oiled, but not the hinges on the door to the Off-Limits Room. These hinges screamed like a woman forced to stick her hand in boiling water. Even though he might easily have flipped on the lights, Max carried a lantern for added suspense. The window was so grimy it provided a nice effect and the kerosene glow of the lantern left the corners suitably shrouded in darkness. A series of magic marker words led the way to a Breaking Wheel, a Coat of Shame, and a Nose Picker. There was a dismembered doll hanging from the ceiling by a meat hook but, by now, Hayden had grown jaded. "It just feels like more of the same."

"Ah, but that's where you're wrong, Mister. Would you dare to judge the Lou-ver without first seeing the Mona Lisa? Or visit Disney World and skip the Pirates of the Caribbean? I think not! Well, here it is, ladies and gentlemen, the crown jewel of the museum: the dreaded Fork in the Road."

An enormous pitchfork-shaped shadow climbed the far wall. "The Fork in the Road was discovered in the root cellar of ninety-two year old Bible native, Barton Moonie, after his death in 1989. Seven bodies and a diary were unearthed less than two miles from this very place. According to his notes, Moonie's victims were strapped into the seat and asked to choose their fate by turning a lever; one direction spelling freedom, the other a fork to the head. In his diary, Moonie claimed the most essential part of the Fork in the Road was giving the victim time to labor over the decision. Four people died of fright before they ever touched the lever. Do you see these little words here on the handle?"

"Yes."

"*Fiat Voluntas Dei*. That's Latin for 'May God's will be done'."

Hayden swallowed and the sound echoed around the Off Limits Room.

"I only wish I could tell you the secret regarding the Fork in the Road. Alas, I'm bound by ethics to hold my tongue."

"Secret?"

"Much like magicians, there are tricks of the trade that one must never divulge. Anyway..." Max made a bow. "This concludes your tour of *The Maxwell Treat Museum of Torture for Young Girls and Boys*. Don't forget to stop by our gift shop."

At first, Hayden barely heard this part; he was busy inspecting the crown jewel of the museum — a pitchfork suspended over a chair of torn plaid. Then it hit him. "Hey, don't I get my name in there somewhere, too?"

Max rearranged his index cards. "It was my idea.

Without me, there'd be no museum."

Hayden shrugged. He didn't care anyway. "Are you really going to have a gift shop?"

"Are you kidding? I've been making gallows out of toothpicks since I was a boy of four. I've got enough merchandise to fill Wal-Mart."

There was only one thing Hayden had in common with his cousins, and that was an above average interest in Minor's speech therapist: a wiggly woman with long blonde hair, a blue angel tattoo, and the improbable name of Miss Butter. Miss Butter was delicious. She came every Wednesday at ten sharp, beeping her horn three times in the drive to signal her arrival. If you ran to her car fast enough, you'd get to carry her picture cards and puppets, a job guaranteed to earn a boy a nice pat on the head. While the Treats excelled at talents like growing mould, dragging out burps, and retooling devices meant for destroying the soles of feet, Hayden's gift was speed. He'd been the fastest runner in grade eight back at Pleasant Valley Middle School and this proved a handy skill when it came to Miss Butter. In fact, he was so quick on his feet that the brothers developed a new obsession: Beat Hayden.

The first couple of weeks, Hayden easily beat everyone to Miss Butter's car, because he'd caught the Treats off guard. Once the boys put their energy into outsmarting him, however, running fast wasn't good enough. Hayden realized what he was up against the morning he discovered his Sketchers nailed to the floorboards in the front hall at nine fifty-five.

"Heh-heh," Max said, sticking his tongue out at Hayden even as Miss Butter gave him an appreciative pet.

Sad to say, carrying Miss Butter's stuff was the high point of Hayden's week. The following Wednesday, he waited on the roof and jumped in front of her bumper before she had chance to beep.

"Heh-heh," he said to Max, who had been too busy setting fire to Hayden's shoes on the porch to get his hands on Miss Butter's puppets.

There were worse things in Hayden's life than guillotines and hopeless love. Every night, the scream of a train whistle ploughed through the black landscape of his dreams as he tossed on his couch bed. The entire house rattled with the approach of something he could never quite see. Clutching his covers under his chin, he'd stare into the darkened family room and watch the beginning of the same dim movie over and over again: an incomplete scene starring his parents and a beam of white light.

Did they forget he was waiting for them that night? Three spoons on the counter lined up and ready to dig into a new tub of Cherry Garcia. The next Family Movie Night movie on the list, *Back to the Future,* already scratched off with a Sharpie. *Apples to Apples* set up on the coffee table, just in case *Back to the Future* turned out to be better when Mom and Dad were kids than it was now. Like *Footloose.* He was twelve years old and didn't have anything better to do on a Saturday night yet, so he was watching TV and waiting for ice cream when the police came to the door.

Now, all his nights were exactly the same. He'd toss and turn and hold his breath as his father prepared to gun it. DON'T DO IT, DAD! he'd plead. And then, he'd feel the Cheerio dust and the cat hair seeping out of the couch cushions and he'd remember he was in Bible now and that they'd failed to think of him, again.

Sometimes, he could stop the train by thinking of Miss Butter's angel tattoo. Other nights, Aunt Tawny would sink down beside him on the couch and pat his back. Together, they would listen to the clicking, snapping, hammering sounds coming from the garage. "I wish I had their energy," she might say.

Uncle Tommy would shuffle into the kitchen, scratching his butt, and maybe make himself a peanut butter sandwich or a Pop-Tart. "Shoot. I wish I had their brains."

Weird as they were, Hayden couldn't imagine his aunt and uncle choosing the thrill of out-running a train over a long happy life with their boys.

"I have bad news," Aunt Tawny told them one morning over breakfast. "Miss Butter won't be able to come on Wednesdays no more."

Three forks clanked against three china plates hard enough to cause chips.

"Why?" Hayden said.

"Schedule conflict, but don't worry. We'll get Miss Butter another day."

Later that week, they were throwing garbage around the stocks to make things look more Elizabethan when Merk said, "You really got it bad for that speech therapist, don't you, Hayden?"

"I knew better girls in California," Hayden lied.

"I bet she'd melt if you kissed her," Merk said. "Get it?

Like butter."

"Forget Miss Butter," Max said. "We're onto something really big here."

"People do love pain," Merk said.

Hayden snorted at this. "Not me."

"That's on account you ain't played the game yet," Max told him.

Hayden dumped a bag of apple cores around the kid-sized stocks. "What game?"

"The Execution Game," Merk said. "We're going to play it today. Max is going to be the executioner and we get to be the condemned."

"I want to be an axe murderer," Minor said.

"You're always an axe murderer," Merk complained. "Why don't you be a Christian for once?"

Minor stuck out his lower lip. "No."

"You could be a saint," Merk coaxed. "I'm going to be St. Anthony the Abbot, the patron saint of skin diseases. Do you want to be a saint, Hayden?"

Max pulled on a black hood. "Hayden's gonna be Hannibal the Cannibal."

"Fffat's not fair," Minor said. Minor had 'defective tongue tip control'.

"Silence!" Max ordered. "You will all be sentenced according to your sins. Minor Treat, please step forward."

Minor happily leapt from the ranks. "You have been charged with murdering folks with an axe. As punishment for your foul deeds, you are hereby ordered into the guillotine." He pushed Minor against the teeterboard and tilted him horizontal.

"That can't be safe," Hayden said.

"Quiet you, or I'll remove your tongue!"

"That guillotine is old," Hayden said.

Max swiped the air with a Swiss army knife, the fish-scaler open and glinting evilly.

Merkle laughed. "I'd like to see you lop off Hannibal Lecter's tongue."

"Grrrrrr," Max said, thrusting the scaler first at Hayden, then at Merkle. "Do you have any last words, Minor Treat?"

Minor spat.

"Very well then, prepare to meet your maker."

Max reached for the handle and Hayden shut his eyes, imagining poor Minor's head squirting like a grapefruit.

Ching!

Hayden heard a gasp — a gurgle — a wooden thud.

Something rolled against his foot. Merk let out a scream. Hayden kept his eyes shut tight. Each heartbeat exploded like a cannon in his chest.

"Poor Minor," Merk wailed. "He couldn't even say his 'th' sounds."

Swallowing hard, Hayden opened his eyes. There it was, malformed and gooshy.

Wrinkly and rotten. "Grapefruit?"

The brothers laughed their butts off. "You're so easy, Hayden."

"I'm leaving," Hayden said.

Maxwell's beefy fingers dug into his arm. "You ain't going anywhere until I execute you, mister."

Hayden had no intention of sticking his head in a guillotine.

"Hannibal Lecter, for the crime of eating things you ain't supposed to eat, I sentence you to the...Fork in the Road."

"But that's my favorite," Merk objected.

"I'm saving The Gunner's Daughter for you, Merkle."

Merkle did a little Touch-Down dance. "Thank you,

Jesus!"

"To the fork," Max shouted, leading them off to the Off Limits Room. Merk fired up the lantern.

"Forget it," Hayden said. "I'm not getting in that thing."

Maxwell checked his watch. "Do you still want to know the secret behind the Fork?"

"I thought you had too much ethics to tell?"

"If you'll get in, I'll make an exception."

Hayden examined the keyhole in the buckle. He was a little curious.

Max checked his watch as if there was a time limit on his decision. "There are only three people alive who know the secret. After today, there could be four." Merk clucked like a chicken. Minor clucked too. Max dangled the key to the buckle in front of Hayden's nose. "Well?"

Hayden flopped down on the sagging cushion. "Ew, it smells like dead cats."

Max put the key in the keyhole. "Prepare to meet your fate!" With that, he gave the key a twist.

Just then, three beeps came from the drive. "Miss Butter!" they cried, dashing to the window.

Max dropped the key in his pocket and smiled. "Heh-heh."

There was a clot of hair stuck to one of the tines. Hayden knew this because they were four inches from his face. He planned to throw up on Max when the first minute they let him out.

It was Monday, not Wednesday. The little sneaks must have learned the therapist's new schedule and planned accordingly. Staring out the dirty window, he watched them disappear in the house with beautiful Miss Butter.

An hour passed. It felt like a year. Hayden sat still as death. He barely breathed. Finally, the boys burst out the front door, laughing and showing off. Miss Butter gave them each a pat on the head and drove off.

The boys went back in the house.

"Hey!" Hayden yelled, wiggling so hard, a tine grazed his forehead. "Hey!"

The lantern worried him. Max said it added drama, but what if they meant to leave him in the Fork all night? He thought of the rat droppings that pebbled the floor. "Hey!" he yelled.

A cheery thought occurred to him: Aunt Tawny wouldn't stand for this. Hayden watched the front door hopefully. Any minute now, they'd fly outside, Aunt Tawny whipping their backsides with her chili pepper dish towel. Another fifteen minutes ticked by before Hayden remembered that Aunt Tawny had taken Uncle Tommy for a root canal.

"Let me outta here!" he hollered, but there was no one to hear. He was too restless to sit still. He rattled the machine, thinking he might be able to shake the old thing apart. In his fury, Hayden kicked over the lantern.

At first it only sputtered a little and licked an oily rag. Then a nearby noose sizzled as it caught fire. Hayden pulled at the buckle and screamed. When no one came out of the house, he turned his attention to the lever.

No.

He didn't want to choose! The tines bobbed before his face, their dull tips blackened with the gooey evidence of a hundred wrong choices. "Help me!" Hayden screamed.

The fire was like a little orange squirrel jumping from branch to branch, only in this case it jumped from index card to index card, eating Maxwell's tour spiel as it went.

The machine was rickety as sin. Perhaps it didn't even work? What if he chose correctly and the fork didn't swoop, but the lock didn't open either?

Fiat Voluntas Dei. May God's will be done.

The wall was burning now. Black smoke curled around him. He looked at the lever. What if he chose wrong? What if the fork skewered him like a meatball, but didn't kill him right off? It would hurt having it stuck in his face like that.

"Help!"

He tried holding his breath. His eyes hurt. He looked at the lever. Much as he was loathe to do it, he relived his parents' final moments once more as the time to make his own decision drew closer and closer...

For the five hundredth time, the Nissan sped toward the crossing in a death race with a train. The Blockbuster bag sat on Mom's lap. Cherry Garcia perspired on the floor. There was some New York Super Fudge Chunk, too. But this time, something seemed different. Dad looked at Mom, but his face didn't flash with light. Nothing whistled. The red and white arm of the crossing signal pointed up at the heavens.

Could it be?

Could it be that there was no warning? No whistle? No stupid last minute decision? Maybe they'd hopped in and buckled up, unaware they were making any decision at all, because they trusted that things would be okay. Whistle or no, maybe God or Fate or plain Dumb Chance decided the matter for them.

God's will be done.

I was always going to come to Bible, Hayden thought with a jarring sense of surprise. I was always going to sit in this chair. Out loud, he said, "The decision, in essence, has already been made."

It was this thought that spurred him into action. He twisted the lever right without giving it anymore thought. Right for his mom, the only right-handed person in the family. Right because a fork went on the left side of a plate. Right, because this seemed as good a choice as any.

Click.

The fork groaned. Hayden flinched. The buckle opened.

He crawled from the burning museum, blind and choking, as five years' worth of toothpick gallows embedded themselves in his palms. Under a sign that read *You Are Here*, the Treat boys descended upon him. "Gosh, Hayden! Did you have to burn up all our stuff?"

Hayden blinked through the poisonous smoke. "This secret of yours better be good, Maxwell Treat."

"Secret?" Max said.

"To the chair!" Hayden was coughing his lungs up by now. The least Max could do was tell him the stupid secret.

"Oh right. It's really rather brilliant, you see. The decision is the entire torture. No matter which way you turn the lever, that old machine is going to set you free either way. Of course, no sooner would one of Moonie's victim's break out of the Fork when he'd throw them down the All's Well that Ends Well well, but I couldn't get my hands on that contraption." He gave Hayden a punch. "I can't believe you torched my life's work."

A fire truck roared up right then and began putting out the flames.

"It's lucky for you, I've always been fascinated by cockroaches," Max said. "Would you believe it? There ain't a decent cockroach museum for a hundred miles around."

Friar Garden, Mister Samuel, and the Jilly Jally Butter Mints

In order to understand the altogether unbelievable and sometimes perfectly dreadful power of a Jilly Jally Butter Mint, one must first understand my sister, Estrella Calliope June-Bug Padora. She sounds odd, I know, especially the June-Bug part, which she made up and gave herself as her *middle* middle name.

Don't ask.

The important thing to know is this: Estrella is not an idiot and she is not an imbecile. We had her tested a few years ago and, good news! Estrella is a moron. Dr. Clumpette says she has the brain of an eight year old, but that's not so awful, is it? Clumpette has seen worse.

My name is Esme Padora, plain and simple. No middle. No *middle* middle. I like it that way. I've been related to Estrella since I was born but, even so, I didn't have much interest in her until the day she reached in her pocket and tossed a fistful of lady's mantle pips into mine and Sam Bell's faces. Flower seeds aren't supposed to twinkle, but these did. We both itched our noses and sneezed and sneezed as though the seeds were part ordinary and part something else entirely.

"Caught you!" Estrella said, blowing one last improbable sparkle straight for our heads. After that, Sam and I didn't go anywhere without her.

Sam, I should say, was Miss Judith's son and Miss Judith was Mom's nurse. He and I were great friends. Estrella wished to be friends too, so she pushed him up against the hazel tree and began separating sparkles from the freckles on his nose with the tip of a wet finger.

"Just like Breezy Boy!" she said of Sam's hair, Breezy-Boy being the palomino pony our father should never have bought her.

Sam was one of those people with tell-tale ears and his tell-tale ears were a hot, wild red the day Estrella caught him. I always thought they were a real hindrance but, it turns out, the ears were nothing. In time, it would be shown that Sam Bell's single greatest misfortune was the fact that he was a boy.

"Would you like to smoke?" Estrella asked us, after she grew tired of rubbing slobber around on Sam's face.

I could scarcely believe my ears. Estrella was a lot of things, but she was not usually a rule-breaker.

"Sure," we said, quick as you please, because Sam and I were a lot of things and rule-breakers were at the tip top of the list.

"Goody," Estrella said. "We're going to catch Dragon Hornets today!" With that, she pulled a canning jar out of mid-air.

"Dragon Hornets?" Sam said.

Estrella opened the jar and pivoted on one toe. In seconds, the whole garden reeked of damson jam. "They only come round the first time someone eats a Jilly Jally, so we mustn't miss our chance."

Sam looked to me for an explanation.
"She's special," I said.
"Very," Sam agreed.
Then Estrella brought out the mints.

Sam and I were fourteen back then; that summer marking the first of many that Mom would claim to be on her death bed. Estrella was sixteen.

Which brings me to this: My father once said that if three friends stand under an umbrella together, one of them is sure to get wet. He and I tend to think alike when it comes to being suspicious but, if I had the chance to do it all over again, I'd change all that. "Ignore the umbrella blither blather," I'd say to me, and that's just one of many things I'd tell myself, if only I could go back.

Here are some others:

Never catch a Dragon Hornet with your bare hands.

Avoid sleeping with Spartans and/or elephants at all cost.

This goes double for mermaids.

Most important of all, if someone should ever happen to offer you a Jilly Jally Butter Mint, say "No, thank you!" Run away and don't ever look back. Keep on running until the day you die.

"Would you like a mint?" Estrella said.

Sam looked at me and I shrugged.

We both held out our hands. "Yes, please."

His was green and mine was pink. We counted to three and kicked them back at the very same second.

"Buttery," Sam said.

"Minty," I said.

"Stick out your tongues," my sister said, and she pushed our faces over Epiphany Pool until our hair dipped in the water.

Sam had eaten a green mint, yet his reflection revealed a tongue pink as a rose. My tongue was green all the way down my throat.

"How can that be?" I wanted to know.

Estrella said, "Don't ask."

We were in Friar Garden, I forgot to say. Friars used to pray there — that's the reason for the name. It was a brambly, knotty, tangled-up place full of all sorts of little hand-painted signs telling you how to find Vesper Rock and Rock of Ages Rock and Testimonial Trail. Epiphany Pool had a sign too, except it was so old, Sam and I had no trouble at all scraping off the "l" one afternoon when there was nothing better to do.

It was commonly believed the birds in the garden built their nests with the old Cincture knots the friars wore to remind themselves of their commitment to poverty, chastity, and obedience. Not a very comfortable bed, if you ask me, but everyone thought it a sacred place. From the start, Sam Bell and I delighted in defiling Friar Garden, carving perverse words on tree trunks with his Wharncliffe whittler, and practicing a made-up form of witchery that involved mixing wizard spells with DeLaMano's magic tricks. It's fitting the Dragon Hornets came to us there.

Estrella said; "Before we begin, you have to say one thing that's a problem for you and promise to turn it into something good. Otherwise, there can be no magic."

"One thing?"

Picking one thing that was a problem for me was a test all by itself. In the interest of getting the ball rolling, however, I dug down deep. I came up with a good one, too. "I'm hopeless when it comes to sharing."

Estrella nodded because she knew it was true. I'd broken a Pete the Pup doll once rather than let her have it for an hour. A penny bank as well.

"Sometimes," Sam admitted, "I'm too sneaky for my own good."

I patted him on the back. "Nice choice! I'd have gone with fibber for you, but you really are a dreadful sneak."

"And I should not drink Moxie soda pop," Estrella declared, slipping her finger inside her nose and pulling out a sparkle. "It makes me burp."

So there they were. Our spiritual tests (some more spiritual than others), a string of sins laid out like knots tied around a friar's girth. Our own Rule of St. Francis, if you will, as stated on the mossy Rule of St. Francis Stone I leaned my hip against:

> *A stern Christian always remembers:*
> *The necessity of penance.*
> *The danger and punishment for vice.*
> *The honor and reward of virtue.*

Never mind Sam and I had long-since scratched his favorite curse *ball-licker* over *Christian* with a stolen salad fork. The mints would lead the way, or so my sister promised. We would enter the garden like our holy brothers before us, and seek to change ourselves.

See how noble it all was?

The word "burp" acted as a signal. After that, the Hornets came. They were the size of a walnut and scaly with four sets of wings and they flew very, very fast. The first Hornet zipped past Sam's ear and I reached up with my hand at the same moment that Estrella scooped in with her jar.

"Caught you!" Estrella said, slamming on the lid.

"Ouch!" I said. A blister popped up on my first

knuckle. "It stung me."

"Oh dear," Estrella said. "That will never go away, either." She gave the wound a kiss. "Better?"

Somehow it was.

"Catch them with this," she said, giving me her jar.

Sam and I fogged up the glass, looking at the angry bug.

"What's coming out of its mouth?" Sam asked.

"Fire," Estrella said, rolling her eyes like we were the ones with feeble minds. "Tonight, Mister Samuel will put the jar by his bed and he'll have a funny surprise in the morning." Mister Samuel is what my sister called Sam.

The little beasts proved irresistible. Once I managed to snag one, Sam had to snag one, too. You have to be fast though when there's fire involved. More than once, we splashed into Epiphany to put out our smoking sleeves. Estrella singed off part of her hair.

Daddy liked to say, "If you play with fire, expect to get burned." I wish I'd listened to that one. Soon, the jar was too hot to touch and whirling with little clouds of steam. After an hour of jumping around, we'd only caught one Hornet a piece. Still, it seemed those few were enough to burn up their little glass world.

Estrella wrapped a muslin pleat around the jar and carried it back to the porch with her dirty knee showing. My hand throbbed like the devil.

"I'm going to look them up in *Bailey's Guide* tonight," Sam said.

Estrella smiled at that.

Earlier that afternoon, we'd been wallowing in self-pity, sure the whole day was doomed to be as dull as the day before. Now Sam's shoe laces had been turned to cinders and I had a hole in my new apron.

"Isn't smoking fun?" Estrella said, dousing her own smoldering apron with a mouthful of spit.

We both agreed it was wonderful. Fantastic! Better than tobacco — which, incidentally, is exactly what dragon fire smells like.

"Thanks," Sam told Estrella, scratching his golden head. Like me, he was shocked to realize Estrella had potential.

"Don't thank me, Mister Samuel. Thank the Jilly Jallys."

That night, Sam Bell went to bed in his little room in the muggy belvedere on top of our house; the three Dragon Hornets huffing and puffing away on the wardrobe trunk by his bed. He'd looked and looked, he told me later, but there was nothing on fire-breathing hornets in *Bailey's Guide* or *The Exciting World of Insects*.

At breakfast the next morning, he passed me something under the table that I could only explore within the confines of my fist until every bite of my rolypoly had been chewed up and swallowed down. It was smooth like a rock, whatever it was. Bumpy. Molten. It made my blister heat up and sting all over again, yet I didn't drop it. I wanted it, despite the pain. I held it tight inside my palm.

Come what may.

"Could I be excused, Daddy?" I said when my plate was clean.

He nodded.

"Mom?" Sam said.

"Go on then, but don't forget the chimneys."

Washing the chimneys on the kerosene lamps was Sam's most dreaded chore, but he didn't even grumble. We ran out the door so fast, Miss Judith and Daddy actually noticed one another, which was not normal, if you must know, seeing as Daddy read the *Wilt Dailey*

Reporter each morning and Miss Judith was just the nurse.

Out in the yard, I opened my hand and looked at the little rock. "What is it?" I whispered.

Sam took his treasure back and held it up to the sun.

Inside the bubbly lump of glass, the three little fire-breathers looked back at me like mosquitoes trapped in a drop of amber, their tiny wings melted to goo.

Oddly enough, the day before was already fading to a furry blur and we got headaches just thinking about Estrella Calliope June-Bug Padora. It felt as though someone had peeled open our skulls and stuffed them like pillows until our fool brains got lost in the fluff. Sam and I spent the better part of the morning checking the undersides of wormy stones, kicking the petals off snowdrops, and furiously mashing anything that turned out to be a toadstool.

"I don't understand it," Sam whined. "There must have been ten Hornets here yesterday."

Over and over again, we reminded ourselves what Estrella said about the Hornets coming only once. Still, it put us in a foul mood to find the magic gone.

"Do you think it's because of me?" Sam asked. "I'm prowling for dragons when I should be cleaning chimneys."

"That's probably it," I said.

At noon, my father yelled for me. Sam's Mom yelled too. I was sure he was in a fix for neglecting the chimneys, but when we ran inside, my father held up my apron and wiggled his finger through the hole. "Explain."

Miss Judith had taken to doing the laundry and she said our clothes stunk of Dill's Best Cut and what did we have to say about that?

Well! I looked my father right in the eye and Sam looked his mother right in the eye and, together, we proceeded to unreel one whopping fish-tale of a fib. They let us get all twisted up in it too, before Daddy slapped his briar pipe down on the table and put an end to that. "I found this in your sister's pocket."

Sam and I, it should be said, had the ability to communicate without so much as a word, a nod, or a scratch of the ass passing between us. This being the case, I opened my hand behind my back and, just like that, Sam slid something into my fingers.

"Have a look at this," I said.

Blister juice ran down my fingers as Daddy held it up to the window. "What am I looking at?"

"Dragon Hornets, sir."

Sam and I exchanged a proud look, waiting to be congratulated on our big discovery. Daddy was a botanist. He had a winter propagator named after him; the wholly inedible, spiky-balled Padora Bramble Nut. Maybe they would name the Hornets after Sam and me? I knew exactly what we would call them...

"Horse shit!" Daddy declared. "Must you always lie, Esme?" No matter how he held the glass, the dragons looked like dirt to him. Consequently, he bent me over the sideboard for a strapping, and Miss Judith let him bend Sam over, too.

To block the pain of what was about to come, I made myself focus on the badminton scar that weaved along the curve of Sam's chin as we stood there shoulder to shoulder, waiting. You could scarcely see the scar by this point, unless you wanted to. I thought of the way it bled in a criss-cross pattern all over his shirt the day our class backhanded him with their rackets. Even Ralph Smallwood gave Sam a whack, and Ralph was one to know about the sting of such things. Before this, Sam and

I had been strangers eating at the same breakfast table, but when the mob ran off and I saw him there with his checkerboard chin and his cold angry eyes, I gave him a hand up.

"Ball-lickers," he said.

I peeled the *Whore Spawn* sign off his back, plucked a shuttlecock from his hair, and decided Sam Bell was my kind of boy. From then on, he was all mine.

When the strap came for me, Sam licked his lips, gave a nod, and grit through the blows right along with me. Then it was his turn. Sweat broke out all over his checkerboard. He clenched his teeth. I gave him the same nod. The crack of leather that followed hurt more than my own whipping.

Ŏ

You might think we'd never be dumb enough to eat Jilly Jallys again.

You'd be wrong.

Ŏ

The next day, Sam and I found Estrella picking a bouquet of wake robins by the workshop. When I say "workshop," you probably picture an old shed full of mud-caked trowels and dusty jars of rat poison. Daddy's workshop was a gingerbread cottage. Star jasmine tendriled through the fretwork and a snowy cloud of Bristol fairy kept the path a secret so that the only regular visitors were the white woods and the moorhens. From the outside, you'd never guess it was the headquarters of Brother Paul's Triply Blessed Liver Suppositories.

Other such enterprises might have been guarded over by a full-time watchman or a half-dozen snapping hounds. My father entrusted his life's work to a nodding batch of cup-and-saucer flowers and an ancient stable door. With the exception of Friar Garden, it was the only part of Sheepsfold left intact from the priory days.

Somewhere, within those cobbled walls, lay the cure for soft heads and aching bones, Daddy was sure of it. "One of these days, I'll fix them both," he vowed. This was why we'd moved to Sheepsfold in the first place: to save my sister and my mother from their afflictions. But don't let the flowers and the moorhens fool you. Peeking in the window was crime enough to make Daddy rip off his belt.

"We'd best keep away from here," I warned Estrella.

In actuality, there was little danger. Daddy was off to Chipping Norton for the day to meet with Edgar Carey, the face behind Brother Paul. On weekdays, Mr. Carey put on a scapular and rosary and went about laying hands on people, touting 'Holy Vinegar for the Hopeful'. "It's good on cod, too!" Mr. Carey liked to say. Daddy thought him a buffoon, but sales were up. On this particular day, he was bringing Brother Paul a fresh supply of vinegar so the "ministry" might be expanded to Cubitt Town.

Estrella slid a bloom behind my ear and reached into her pocket. Somehow, my simple-minded sister managed to get her hands on the key to Daddy's workshop. Before I could grab the thing, however, she shut it in her fist. "First, we have to eat a mint."

"No thank you, dear. Give me the key."

"Don't worry, Esme. The Dragon Hornets won't be back. This time, we'll just float around."

I laughed at that.

The cups-and-saucers froze on their stalks.

Estrella opened the door, and raced inside. Sam and I followed.

"Gosh," Sam said, spinning in circles as he looked

around the place. Electrical wires spanned the room, looping doorknobs and curtain rods before diving frayed-head first into a cloudy pickle jar; a jar which, upon closer inspection, contained a pickled fetus. "That's not fair," Sam said, because we didn't have electric in the house.

On the shelves, medical books flopped open beside *Ridley's Work on Herbs*. Honeysuckle shared a dish with mouse droppings. Mason jars were home to "Female Complaints", "Venereal Warts", and "Diarrhea".

I must warn you not to confuse Dr. Pierce and his nasal douches with what my father was doing. Daddy truly believed in better living through medicine. He bought Sheepsfold for Friar Garden after he learned it was the only place in the world where hogswallow grew. Mom had yet to come down with the sore joints that would send her to bed screaming, but Daddy was sure he could cure Estrella. He sold his remedies to fund his work, choosing the name Brother Paul after discovering that medicines like Fast Back-Fixer failed to pull in the business.

Daddy didn't care about Brother Paul and his interests ran well beyond the normal ailments Dr. Pierce targeted. My father sold something called Blessed Peace of Mind, a concoction of Solomon's seal and prune juice that, when taken twice daily for a week, could help a man make difficult decisions. The only thing phony about Peace of Mind from Daddy's point of view was the "blessed" part. His most popular nostrum that year was a pill that made your nose bleed if your lover was being untrue.

"Look up," Estrella said.

We looked up at the rafters two stories above. A ratty cobweb waved at us.

"I wrote my name by that nest up there."

She pointed.

We squinted.

"That could be an 'E'," Sam allowed.

"Or bird doot," I said.

Estrella held out the mints. "Float up and see for yourself."

It was impossible, of course. The ceiling was ridiculously high.

Still.

This time around, I took the green and Sam took the pink, but, when we stuck out our tongues afterward, I was still the green one.

"I don't seem to be floating," I told Estrella.

"You have to wait for the blackbirds."

Then it started.

"Wheee!" Estrella cried. At first, I only saw her pink toes wiggling as they lifted off the floor. Her arms were out, but dangling at the elbows, and a long curl of hair was sticking up off the top of her head. She smiled like an angel as she went. I held up my arms and waited.

Nothing happened.

"Ow!" Sam hissed, but he was going up too, and now I could see why. Two birds clipped him like clothespins, pinching separate tufts of hair on opposite sides of his head. I should have died laughing, if I weren't so horrified. Another bird swooped in and pecked up a shoulder seam. Still another went for the seat of his britches. Bottom out, Sam rose and rose, whisked heavenward by his horns.

"I don't like this," Sam said.

"Make it stop, Estrella!" I demanded. I grabbed for Sam's foot as he swung by, but he was already beyond my reach.

"Relax," Estrella said. By now, the birds had made a

maypole of her head, circling with ribbons of hair. A bird fluttered up the bell of her dress and bit down on one of the beads Estrella wore around her ankle. It flew aloft, anklet in beak, drawing her foot up as it went.

You've never seen such grace.

Birds gathered at her elbows, her buttons, a bow at her waist, and here's the strangest part of all: every blackbird was white.

"Close your eyes, Mister Samuel, and hold out your hand."

Sam was still kicking, but he did as she said. Damned if his birds didn't fly over to Estrella's birds and deliver his hand to hers. "Don't be afraid," she said.

The birds seemed too busy to bother about me and I wasn't completely sorry. "Does it hurt?" I asked, wanting to hear that it did.

"I'm okay," Sam said.

"We need more birds," Estrella called down. "I'll eat another mint."

I was never one to miss out, but I might have been willing this time, had there not been so much laughter going on up there. In Sam's effort to hold on to Estrella, he'd scratched her arm and yanked the buttons off her sleeve, sending them raining down on my head. The way those two carried on, you'd think they'd never seen anything so funny as buttons bouncing off my face.

Estrella ate another mint and the birds came for me at last, appearing as if such creatures could squeeze up through floorboards or rise from a Petri dish — albino blackbirds, gold rings around their eyes and jaws as strong as hedge-clippers.

To properly picture this, you need to know that my sister had been born with hair like no other. Mermaid hair that yielded gifts from within like lost paperclips or pebbles that glitter when you hold them in the sun. Fig

Newtons were known to pile up in there. Once, she shook her head and a little brown toad tumbled out. Sometimes, Estrella's tresses seemed to writhe of their own accord, like octopi, and it was a known fact that certain pale strands were green all summer long and turned pumpkin orange in November.

I do not have mermaid hair. It is not green or orange. It holds no hidden treasure. Should birds decide to pluck at it, there's every chance I'd go bald. I mention this to show what a brave soul I am.

Fortunately, I was bound upward by a cuff, an apron string, and both of my boot laces. It could not have been pretty, but I got to keep my hair. There was no enjoying the ride up, however, until Estrella and Sam each grabbed a wrist and drew me into the circle.

"Look!" Estrella said, jerking her head at the dove's nest. "I told you I wrote my name up here."

Estrella had written more than her name:

Estrelah Calowpee Jun Bug Padoorah Luvs Mester Samule

"She doesn't know what she's saying," Sam reminded me later when we were doing the chimneys. The Franciscan order had left behind an aviary and this was where we did the job. We'd pluck a dirty lamp from the seed hopper, give it a quick scouring, and leave it on a nest box to dry.

"You better be careful, Sam." I'd seen his ears when he read my sister's misspelled declaration. "You're flattered that she likes you."

"Don't be stupid." He reached in the neck of a chimney, grunting as he scrubbed.

"She doesn't call you Bastard Boy like all of the other kids do, so maybe you like her, too?"

Some towns, I should think, have plenty of bastards to

go around, but Wilt had only one and Sam was it. Poor Sam. Everyone liked him perfectly fine until word got out that he had no father. God as my witness, if there had been an easier way to make friends, I should never have whispered the truth to a big mouth like Ralph Smallwood.

"Go to Hell," Sam said. He had a smudge on his nose, but I didn't tell him that. Let him walk around all day with a dirty nose. It would serve him right for dropping buttons on my head!

The reason Sam loathed the chimneys was this: he hated how people would walk out of a room and leave a lamp burning, the insides growing scorched and black for no practical reason. The mess was worth it, Sam said, if you were burning it to see. Otherwise, you were just dirtying things up for nothing.

I thought of Sam twirling through the rafters with Estrella and I worried he was going to burn up all for nothing.

○

"Where do you get the Jilly Jallys?" I asked my sister after I'd washed my hands of Sam for the day. Estrella was swinging on the garden swing and I was pushing. Sam had stalked off to his room to paint.

It was Sam's dream to go to art school someday. He had a tray of Winsor & Newton tubes and four sable brushes and that was all, so he painted the walls in his room over and over again. The belvedere was his Sistine Chapel. As I pushed Estrella high into the cherry leaves, I pictured Sam painting knives in my eyes across the dome of his Sistine Chapel.

"Come on. I'll show you," Estrella said, kicking the branches and leaping off. Pink blooms settled in her hair.

A startled butterfly emerged on sulfur wings.

Estrella skipped all the way to Froggiedale, which is what we called her room. She collected every kind of frog there was: carved frogs, stuffed animal frogs, porcelain frogs. I had to step on frogs to get to her bed. At that particular moment, the night table was peppered with Jilly Jally Butter Mints. They rolled under the frog lamp. They spilled on the frog rug. "All I have to do is ask for them when I say my prayers and I wake up with more on my table," she said.

I reached out my hand to take one. "Not now, Esme," Estrella said. "It isn't proper without Mister Samuel."

We ate an awful lot of mints that summer, and yet, my memories crack like a broken mirror whenever I try to get a peek at them. Only fractured pieces remain. Often, I would come into myself with grass in my hair or my feet scratched up, and I wouldn't remember where the scratches came from. Though only a single hour may have passed, I would be left with broken shards instead of whole memories: a cricket crawling across my forehead, a talon on my arm, my face under water. There were more odd creatures too, but sometimes, only the look in their beady eyes stayed clear in my head. Once, I thought I remembered feeling Sam's tongue in my mouth. He tasted like pears. When I woke up the next morning, there was an empty bottle of perry by my bed. "Did you kiss me yesterday?" I asked Sam.

"I'd remember that," he said.

I don't know how many times I turned those words around, poking at them like puzzle pieces you don't know what to do with.

When school started, we were jittery, distracted

students. People still called Sam Bastard Boy, but, this year, a lot of girls were starting to look sorry for him. Estrella was sent off to Miss Litton's School for Educable Morons to learn how to keep out of the workhouse. We missed her more than I can say. Sometimes, we tried praying for Butter Mints, but they never showed up. In October, we turned fifteen.

That same month, Daddy enjoyed a kind of hero-status around town after coming up with a brew of cotton lavender for Constable Langtry who nearly died from a spider bite. Serpent's Bane, Mr. Carey was calling it, and it was flying off the shelves. For all Daddy's efforts though, my mother stayed in her sickroom, growing no better or worse. "Give me another cup of my elixir," she would say, her pupils big as Black Beauty marbles. Looking at her was like looking into a pit. I didn't know my Mom anymore and she didn't know me. Worst of all, she didn't seem to care. I cared, but whenever I got to thinking about it too much, I made Sam go steal a Dairy Milk with me or set a bush on fire.

Shortly before Estrella was due back, I went up to Sam's room and saw the mermaid on his wall. At the time, he was in the corner painting a pool of yellow blood around a crushed beetle, but I didn't give two cents about the blood. I was jealous of Sam's mermaid.

If you'd seen it, this might not sound half as silly as it does when you write it down. It was different than Sam's other stuff. All of his best work was grim. Persians flung themselves on Spartan spathas around his sagging bookshelves. Red-tail hawks devoured snakes on his floor. His specialty was bloody teeth. The mermaid swam amid the carnage, her pale flesh glistening with droplets that sparkled like lady's mantle pip. There was a secret concealed in her right hand, too. It was amazing work. A green tail rippled across two walls. Rainbow hair fanned the dome. Two wet lips blew a kiss at his pillow, aiming for the empty imprint left by his big head. This was his Mona Lisa. His Hamlet. His Ninth Symphony!

"You pig," I said. "You've painted Estrella."

"Look closer."

"I am looking, you pig."

Sam sighed. "Remember when I asked if I could paint you?"

"Don't change the subject." I tried letting Sam paint me once, but it was just too miserably dull. He got mad because I wouldn't sit still and I got mad because he got mad. That's usually how it worked. I shouldn't have cared who he painted on his walls, but it was hard to see my sister wiggling her tail across his bedroom when I was used to having Sam to myself.

"I'd paint you if you'd let me," he said.

"Did Estrella *let* you?" I growled.

"No, but Sara Moody did."

"Sara Moody?" I took a closer look. "I should have recognized that bosom."

"It is nice," Sam said, looking up at Sara's bosom.

"You're in love with Sara Moody now?"

"She let me kiss her."

"So, you had to paint her big as the sky all over your ceiling?"

"Yes, as a matter of fact. It was fun."

"What's in her hand?"

"She brought me a periwinkle from Birkenhead. They went there on holiday."

"The last I knew, she was still calling you Bastard Boy."

He dabbed blood on a mandible. "Well, she likes me now."

I sat on his bed. My eyes teared up. Sam looked at me like I was crazier than Estrella. He rubbed his eyebrow.

He rubbed his chin. His ears lit up. "There," he said, stabbing at my nose with his paintbrush, marking me with a stripe of Cadmium Lemon.

"What are you doing?"

"Painting you." He ran his wet brush across my cheek.

I jumped away.

"Sit still," he said, pressing down on my shoulder hard enough to hurt. The tip of his tongue glided over his lip as he painted ticklish strokes around my mouth. He leaned back to observe the results. "Beautiful," Sam said. He gave me a quick kiss.

Except for maybe, possibly, the time we mixed our mints with perry, Sam had never kissed me before.

"What about Sara Moody?"

His smile was smeared with my mouth paint. "I like her a lot."

"Pig."

"I like you better. We're not kids anymore, Esme."

"We aren't?"

His ears were really fired up now. "When I asked if I could paint you, I had this whole big plan, but you wouldn't sit still. I thought I'd never figure out a way to kiss you, so I gave up. Then, Sara started writing me notes on her Emily Dickinson stationary."

"Emily Dickinson?"

"*My river runs to thee*. That's what it said. Anyway, I thought, maybe I'd kiss her instead."

"You gave up that easily?"

"Does your river run to me?"

"Sara's brain is the size of a pea."

"Do you want to kiss me or not, Esme?"

I rubbed the lemon off his lips. "Let's see." I kissed him. "It's very weird." I tried again. "It feels funny." One more time...

This was a long one.

"I want you to do something for me before we go any farther, Sam."

"Name it," he said.

"Paint my head on that mermaid."

"Okay."

"Leave the bosom. It'll give me something to strive for."

That's how Sam and I started kissing. I loved him more than anything. I always had. Kissing him was weird, funny, and wonderful. By the time Estrella came home, we were doing it a lot and she had to throw more sparkles on us to get a moment of our attention.

The next time I ate a mint, I was surprised to realize how much smaller it looked in my hand. Beneath its melty minty taste, there was a slight flavor of turned cream that I'd never noticed before. Had the mints changed over the last year? Or was it my tongue? I thought of all the wonderful daydreams I'd been having about Dragon Hornets and tried to swallow the bitterness away.

We were sitting in the honeyberries behind the barn. Inside the barn was an empty bridle hook and an unused tin of saddle soap. I found myself wondering if Estrella even remembered about that saddle soap. Or what happened the day Daddy let her ride her new pony to town.

"Be gentle with the Mama Mias," Estrella instructed. "They hurt easily."

"What are Mama Mias?" we asked.

"They're Italian."

Something touched my ankle and I laughed because I thought it was Sam. A vine, red as my burn, began slithering up my shin.

"Mama Mia!" Estrella exclaimed, petting my vine. A red shoot wrapped around Sam's leg, too, and he tried to kick it off. Estrella put her hand on his knee. "Don't fight it, Mister Samuel. It feels good."

Vines were slinking up my skirt, around my waist, and under my arms, to tickle me. My instinct was to fight them, but they moved so sinuously, I quickly lost the will. An hour passed. I remember nothing but the caress of those vines. They stroked shyly. Cleverly. Like human fingers. They covered my eyes with leaves. I lost track of Sam and my sister, but I could hear them murmuring to the vines.

Later, I stumbled from the Mama Mias, dizzy and on fire. This was not like the Dragon Hornets at all. I wanted to be fourteen again, staring into a jar with my mouth dropped open. But I was not fourteen.

"Come here," Sam said, appearing suddenly, one vine still twisting around his foot. He shook it free, pulled me into the barn, and kicked the door shut. Usually he was a nervous kisser, working away at my mouth until the inside was raw for days after, torn up from our teeth. After the vines, he groped me blindly, kissing everywhere. I couldn't see him in the hot black barn, but I could feel him. Somewhere, a horse snorted. Or maybe that was Sam.

Estrella knocked on the door. "I want to come in, too!"

Sam froze for a moment.

"Forget her," I said. We hit one wall, and then another, rattling the soap tin to the ground. I bumped my head on something sharp and Sam kissed the spot as if he knew exactly where I hurt. He breathed my name. *Esme.* I held on tight.

Knock. Knock.

"Don't let her in," I said as I undid his buckle.

"Open up!" a man's voice ordered.

"We were looking for the potato riddle," I told my father.

"Well, leave the door open next time."

I smiled. I thought I was off the hook.

Daddy jerked me by the arm. "Don't make me fire his mother, Esme. Mom needs her too badly."

And, as he stormed away: "I'll expect mashers for supper tonight."

We were done with the mints. We both agreed. If Daddy saw us together for any reason at all, he scowled until we each went to opposite sides of Wilt. The vines had made us lose our heads. Sam and I were a lot of things, but we weren't *that* crazy.

"Maybe next summer," I said, with respect to going crazy.

"Or this winter," Sam said.

"But not now," I told him.

"No, not now," Sam agreed. "Maybe in July."

Sad to say, once you've experienced the Mama Mias, you can't un-experience them.

Estrella followed like a puppy everywhere we went. "Shall we have the Jilly Jallys now?" she always asked. We always said no, but some days were harder than others.

One day, she followed us into Five Choirs Vineyard where ancient grapevines soldiered on amid wild bands of rabbits and weeds. Sam picked a black Barbara and wiped it clean on his shirt. "Eat these instead, Estrella. They're better for you." She ate right from his fingers and licked the juice off his thumb.

"Mister Samuel is yummy," Estrella said. "You should taste him, Esme."

Sam held a grape to my lips. "Taste me, Esme."

The grape was a mix of flavors. Licorice. Plums. Sam. "Delicious," I said.

"He'd go well with a mint," my sister pointed out.

"Let's do it," said Sam. "We could use a little fun."

"No," I insisted. Someone had to be strong. It had been eight days since Daddy caught us in the barn.

"Maybe Mister Sam and I will have one then?" Estrella proposed, and she wasn't even being tricky.

"Yeah," Sam said. "Just because you're a party pooper, that doesn't mean we have to miss out."

All winter, we had longed for Estrella to return and liven up our lives. We dreamt of the mints. Now, I edged up to the boy with the delicious fingers and said: "Don't you dare, Sam Bell."

Before Daddy found out that the nurse he'd hired was bringing along her bastard, the belvedere on the roof was just an open look-out. To make it habitable, he'd put rippled cylinder glass into the windows and cleaned out the dead leaves. Sam could see to Christ's Cross if he squinted hard enough. Best of all, his floor was my ceiling and he could stomp messages to me. I had to climb up on Grammy Fogg's old chain-stitcher and use my church shoe in order to reply, but it worked. Six stomps meant, "I'm bored." Four meant, "Come quickly."

The night after the grapes, I was asleep in bed when I heard: Stomp. Stomp. Stomp. Stomp.

I wasn't to visit Sam's room anymore, but the clock read two a.m. so I decided to risk it. Up the rickety ladder I crept; creak creak creak. Through the creaky door.

Sam ran at me.

My feet left the floor as he twirled me around, giving me a deep kiss. "I can't sleep," he said.

Moonbeams filtered through Daddy's cheap panes, smearing the room like a watercolor. The stiff-spined Spartan on the wall melted into a peaceful Athenian and his sword became a lyre.

"Look what I've got," Sam said, opening his hand.

You might well guess what was in there.

"Did you pray for them?" I asked.

Sam laughed. "Sure I did. Then I reached in Estrella's pocket and grabbed some."

In the old days, I might have appreciated his ingenuity more, but the mints scared me. "I think you ought to toss them out the window this instant."

"No way," Sam said crossly. He sat on the bed and popped one in his mouth. "If you don't want yours, I'll eat them both."

"No!" Good heavens. "When Estrella ate two, we got double the birds." I raised the candy to my mouth. "What if it goes badly without *her*?"

"We're in my room. It's safe enough."

I doubted that. I ate mine anyway. "Estrella always seems to know what's coming," I said.

"I know what's coming," Sam said, and he gave me another kiss. "Wasn't that nice?"

It was. We did it some more.

"The mints aren't working," I said.

Sam kissed my neck while I looked for white blackbirds.

"I don't feel anything. Do you feel anything?"

His lips paused on my throat. "I feel a little something."

I smacked him. "I mean, the mints."

Sam touched the button on my nightgown and looked

into my eyes. "In case you didn't know it: I love you, Esme."

Hm. Actually, I didn't know it. He'd never said so before.

"Do you think we'll get married?" he asked.

"Mints have a funny effect on you."

"It's not the mints," he said. Then he knocked me on the floor.

At first, I only heard the swoosh of the Spartan's sword. Previously that sword had been stuck in an Athenian helmet. Now it dripped blood and brains as it hacked the wardrobe trunk in half. But for that last minute shove from Sam, the sword would have chopped off my head rather than the pineapple on his bedpost.

"Under here," Sam called, pulling me beneath the bed. But there were other evils down there.

A stampede of miniature elephants was taking place across the floorboards. To avoid the little buggers, I had to squeeze up next to a corpse with really nice bloody teeth. Meantime, the spatha was decimating the rest of the room. Flat on our bellies beside the dust bunnies and the corpse, I completely lost my temper, "You should paint nicer things, Sam."

"I didn't know!"

"You should never have taken those mints from Estrella."

The elephants hurt, even if they were small, and I couldn't quite get away from them. They pounded across my shoulder blades, trampling into each other and landing on their tusks. Just when I thought I couldn't take one more horn in my flesh, a voice spoke to us from beyond the mattress.

"Climb on my tail," it said. Shiny green hair reached under the bed and scooped us up like a giant hand.

"Return to your homes, you beasts," the mermaid

said, and, amazingly, the "beasts" obeyed.

Clinging to her paint-chip scales, we shuddered with relief. One heartbeat later, the room was still.

"Be good," she said, setting us on the bed and swimming back up to the ceiling.

"Help me, Esme!" Sam said, grabbing a paintbrush and turning the Spartan's face into a messy Cobalt splotch. "Get the beetle."

But I was staring at the mermaid. "I knew it," I said. "It's Estrella."

Learn! Learn! Learn! I told myself. The mints were bad news! If our run-in with those paintings was not lesson enough, Sam and I had a huge fight afterward.

"Why do you see Estrella's face instead of your own?" Sam shouted at me.

"Why don't you see Estrella's face?" I'd shouted back.

He'd painted the mermaid's eyes green and given her big ears but that didn't make the mermaid me.

"You know what you are, Esme? A jealous, black-hearted ball-licker."

"Sometimes I could really kill you, Sam."

He rammed my face against the shaving mirror. "Stick out your tongue."

"No."

He squeezed my cheeks until I tasted mirror. "Green," he said. "Always green."

"It's the Jilly Jallys."

"Is it?"

"You sleep with Estrella over your bed!"

"Go away," Sam said, pointing at the door. "I don't want to marry you anymore."

"Good!"

"Great!"

Without saying so, we decided never to speak to one another again.

"Tell Sam those chimneys better be done by noon or, I swear, I'll skin him alive," Miss Judith said.

It had been four days. It had been forever. I was tempted to tell Miss Judith that I couldn't tell Sam anything because we were never going to speak again. I was also tempted to keep her threat to myself and let her skin him alive. For a whole ten seconds, I considered doing the chimneys for him. Where was he these days anyway? Except for the mermaid swimming around in blue blotches, his room was utterly empty. He was not in the barn, the privy, or cleaning the chimneys. He was not floating around the workshop.

That left the garden.

Two sets of footprints led me to the vineyard. Maybe it was only the whoosh of moon daisies whipping past my knees, but I thought I heard a ghostly friar warning me to turn back. Then the vines started to giggle. "Mister Samuel is yummy," they said. I peeked through the grape leaves and there they were, my sister and Sam.

He was on his back with his shirt flung open, lying on a bed of pincushion flowers. The tip of his tongue was pinker than the pincushions. Estrella was on her knees beside him. "Mmm," my sister said. She touched her wiggling tongue to his nipple. "Yummy yummy yummy."

To what degree Sam was yummy, I did not wait and see. Fiery tears poured down my cheeks as I tore through the garden. Daisy petals flew in my wake. *He loves me. He loves me not...* "I warned you," the friar said.

It was all ruined now. Sam Bell, the only thing I loved, had been eating mints without me.

He wrapped the Dragon Hornets in Christmas paper and left them on my bed.

I gave them back.

He followed me into the privy.

I slammed the door in his face.

He slid a note in my lap at breakfast.

I burned it unread.

"Talk to me," he begged and begged. "I miss you, Esme. I need you!"

I was a cyclone of fury, whipping around the house. Try as I might, I could not stop blowing. Sam had to physically pin me up against the barn one day, and even then, I continued to roar. "I saw you in the vineyard with Estrella!" I cried, my voice a Herculean wind.

He dropped my wrists he was so surprised. He thought I hated him because of the elephants.

"What did you see?"

"As if you don't know!" I sneered, wanting him to think the worst.

"I don't know, Esme." He slumped in the honeyberries and threw his head against the wall. "I can't remember anything."

"Anything?" I asked skeptically.

He rubbed his eyes. "There are bits and pieces, of course. There always is. We ate some grapes. Estrella tied flowers in my hair."

"You remember more than that because you look scared out of your wits."

"I don't know what I did with her, Esme. That's the

truth. There were grape juice stains all over my stomach afterward, but that doesn't mean I touched her." He held up a palm inked with honeyberry guts to make his point. I smacked his hand away.

"You stupid pig," I said, slumping down beside him.

"You know how it is with the mints, Esme. You know!"

"That's the worst part about it, Sam. You know how it is too, yet you ate one with her anyway."

He stroked my arm with a shaky blue fingertip. "Can you ever forgive me?"

I was no better at forgiving than I was at sharing. I pulled my arm away.

○

When you have a moron for a sister, your father has to like her better and give her a horse whether she deserves one or not, but the sneaky boy you're in love with should not give her anything. Maybe not even friendship. I had to know the truth, one way or another so I went to Estrella.

"He touched my heart," she told me cupping one hand over her breast.

"I'll bet he did."

Things were growing more wretched by the day. Mom was drinking her "elixir" every chance she got. Estrella was wishing for more mints than she could use. Sam and I couldn't look at each other. The garden teemed with fruit and butterflies but, in my mind, the peaches all became Sam's skin and the wood nymphs were Estrella's tongue.

Most days, Sam hid in the belvedere, stomping out messages that I ignored. Some days, I saw them together. Once, he laced her boots for her. Another time, she helped him do the chimneys.

I gave him the cold shoulder for weeks. Months. It was easy when I saw him kneeling at her feet. I read books instead of kissing Sam. I even read to Mum. I'd think of Estrella in the aviary, wiping his smudges with her hair, and my soul would wither all the more. Share my beloved Sam with Estrella? Never! I'd rather not have him at all.

One thought kept running through my head. *If only there was some way to get to the bottom of what really happened that day in the vineyard.*

Then, one morning when school was about to begin, Estrella floated into my room on tiptoe and woke me with a kiss. She stretched and yawned, the buttons on her nightgown straining to reveal little pink ovals of flesh sticking out in between. I ran my hand over her belly. It was hard and small and a little bit round. "Tummy doesn't feel good," she said.

"What's in there, Estrella?"

She poked her bellybutton with her index finger. "Gas bubbles that won't pop."

Sure, it looked like an ordinary case and yet I felt betrayed. When I thought of what else it might be, the feral patter of something cold and dark crept into my head.

For years, I'd been curing Estrella's stomach aches with two spoonfuls of Brother Paul's Amazing Miraculous Release, yet I didn't reach for miracles this time. Instead, I sat Estrella down on my quilt and gave her the velvet pouch of marbles that she so loved to dig through. While Cat Eyes and Aggies clinked together in her hands, I thought about that stupid vow the three of us had made in the garden over mints.

It seemed a long time ago to me now and yet, some things remained unchanged. Sam, the dirty little louse, had made no progress at all. Lord knows, he was as sneaky as ever. Estrella was still bringing gas bubbles on, too. I was the only one who to make a proper attempt at improving myself. I'd tried sharing Sam with Estrella and look where it got me.

"Thank you for sharing," Estrella said. She poured the marbles out onto her aproned lap and ran her fingers through them. "You never let me play with your things."

Alright. So, maybe I was still as selfish as ever. Maybe I only let Estrella come around when it suited my purpose to do so. The three of us were equally pathetic, I decided. No wonder the magic disappeared. I gave myself a hard rap on the head for not trying harder.

Estrella scooped a shiny Oxblood from the pile and held it to her eye. "Pretty!" she said. Quick as that, she popped it into her mouth, hiding it from me on the right side of her jaw.

"Stupid vows," I said out loud. "Who needs magic anyway?"

I led her into the kitchen where my father was reading his *Dailey Reporter* and Sam's Mom was cooking our breakfast. I took his hand off the newspaper and put it on Estrella's stomach. "We should have this checked," I said innocently, fully aware of how bloated Estrella's stomach could get.

My father was not a calm man, but he looked into my sister's eyes and blinked ten times and spoke as kindly as I'd ever heard him speak. "Has a man come into your life, Estrella?"

"Oh yes," she said, thrilled as can be.

Daddy took a very deep breath but still he was calm and kind. "Who is he, June-Bug?"

My sister grinned and clapped her hands. "Mister

Samuel," she said.

Daddy slammed his fist down on the table and made the dishes dance. "Fetch me Dr. Clumpette!" he roared.

After that, things happened in a Jilly Jally way. Sam's Mom burned herself on the frying pan and I felt the pain in my own knuckle and sucked on it to cool it.

It wouldn't cool.

To look at him, you'd think someone had smashed my father with a mallet. "Did he hurt you?" he whispered.

Estrella tapped her finger against her lip as if she were trying to remember. "One time, he pulled off all my buttons, but it only bled a little."

The dishes did another dance.

"Bring the constable, Esme."

Like buttons showering on my face, the magnitude of what I'd done hit me all at once. A year before, there was a man in Wilt accused of raping a girl. He "beat himself to death" in his cell with a baton. At the time, Constable Langtry had called it an unfortunate, but inevitable, outcome, given the circumstances.

I climbed on top of the chain-stitcher and beat my church shoe against the ceiling. I wasn't at all sure if he would come, but he did. "He's sending me for the Constable, Sam. You have to run away."

"The Constable?"

I licked my lips and grit my teeth, waiting for the strap. My strap. His strap. "I'm sorry," I said.

Without a word, a nod, or a scratch of the ass, Sam Bell pulled something from his pocket and put it into mine.

Then he ran.

Constable Langtry creaked up the stairs holding his baton. "You might want to see this," he called down, and we all hurried up the ladder to join him in Sam's room.

That the bedpost was still pineapple-less did not surprise me in the least, nor did the crack in the trunk. What hurt my heart were the blotched walls of the once glorious Sistine Chapel.

Langtry wore a big handlebar mustache that drooped in a permanent frown. He pointed his stick at the ceiling and frowned. "He painted her picture over his bed."

"Look closer," I said. "That's me up there."

Imagine that. In the end, I was the only one who could see my face on Sam Bell's ceiling. Maybe this was because I wanted it to be my face. Or maybe this was because it was mine all along.

You can't diddle a girl who has the brain of an eight year old. That's what Langtry told my father. Estrella was not responsible. Regardless of what happened, my father must press charges.

Watching his furry frown twitch with indignation, I felt certain Langtry wouldn't give a rip about the mysterious powers of Jilly Jally Butter Mints, nor would he care that it was my sister who fed them to us in the first place. At any rate, the constable assured my father, it was no bother to hunt the boy down. "After all," Langtry said. "I owe you my life."

As the constable set off sniffing after Sam, Dr. Clumpette rode up on his mare.

"The doctor wants to have a look at you," I told my sister, helping her into bed. I gave her Greenie Frog to hug and she drank down two teaspoons of Miraculous Release and smiled a milky smile.

When the doctor was done, he called my father back into the room. "This girl is innocent as the day she was born. There are no signs of violation."

"What?" my father said.

"Are you sure?" I said.

"Pop!" Estrella said.

At that same moment, a gun fired. Twice. We ran to the window just in time to see the constable dragging Sam from the garden. Red leaves covered his dirty clothes and one looked bigger and redder than the rest. I cranked open the window. The big leaf was blood.

Instead of seeing Sam lying on the ground, I saw broken banks and dolls with faces cracked by a foolish girl's tantrums. I shook my head hard and it was only then that I saw the boy I loved again. As I watched, the constable bent down to wipe something off Sam's cheek with the tip of his glove. He blew on it and it spiraled away, drifting skyward in a whirlwind of sparkles. Then it disappeared.

"There now," my sister said, knocking over a bottle of Moxie on the table. "My gas bubbles are all gone."

I slid my hand into my apron pocket, expecting to discover Dragon Hornets, but finding a hole instead.

The Reading Lessons

Two minutes after Dr. Mangrove made the announcement that Hadley Crump was going to die, Lucinda walked in the bedroom, stirring a cup of chamomile with her finger and smiling like it was Christmas. Hadley's momma lay across his legs, soaking the blanket with her tears, but Lucinda wasn't one to pay Hadley's momma much mind. She poked that tea-stirring finger in his mouth as though she meant to feed him the whole cup one lick at a time.

"I brought you something," she said, and she wasn't talking about tea. Hadley followed her gaze to the strip of violet paper on the rim of the saucer. He waited until she left to refill the cup before he let himself look at it.

I could hear the churning sound of her tongue as it licked her teeth and lips, and I could feel the hot breath on my neck...

About the time he got to the hot breath part, Hadley's fingers let loose and the words loopty-looped away with all the devilish momentum of a broken promise.

On any other day, Hadley's momma would have been curious to know what Lucinda Browning had passed to her seventeen year old son.

On any other day, Hadley would have squashed the note in his palm, hiding it away like he hid all of Lucinda's secrets.

Lucinda, however, was always on her toes. Because Hadley was the cook's son and Lucinda Browning was a Browning, she was careful to return later and search for the note under his bed. "Did you read it?" she asked.

Hadley gave a nod.

Lucinda balled the note up and pitched it in the fire. With a sigh that seemed to say, *Well that's that then*, she leaned down and ran her teeth around the hair pin-curve of his ear. "Tell me this, Hadley; if you had it to do all over again...would you do it all over again?"

Hadley, who suffered a sudden and desperate desire to do *it* all over again, could only answer, "Yesssssss."

To remember it was to re-live it:

"Hadley Crump. Hadley Crump," Lucinda called out through the twisty tunnel of his memories. Easy as that, Hadley was sucked back. "I'd like to write a poem about you, boy, but the only words I can think of to rhyme with Hadley are "badly" and "madly" and those are awfully sordid words to use for a *child*."

"How about 'gladly'?" the child suggested. The day Hadley was remembering happened when he was nine years old.

Lucinda Browning was nine as well, but her mouth was at least twenty.

"Have these washed," she said, throwing her bloomers in his face. "And I better get them back."

Hadley stood there with her underwear on his head as she composed the Hadley poem:

There once was a boy named Hadley
Who wanted a girl very badly
She was out of his reach
But he hung on like a leech
Loving her gladly and madly.

Seeing how he was only nine, Hadley thought it just plain nuts that he would ever love any girl other than his momma. Even so, the bloomers made his brain swirl to such a degree, he grew convinced the poem was some sort of witchy incantation. Lucinda's underwear smelled of Sweetheart soap and sunshine. Hadley got to like them so well that he thought he might never take those sunshiny knickers off his head.

"Worm!" She snorted, yanking them away, but there was something familiar about the bright fired-up eyes that glared into his own. They were the same eyes Uncle Orv wore right before he gobbled up that plate of fat pullets and choked himself dead at the table.

And, seeing how he was only nine, Hadley promptly forgot about those sweet-smelling bloomers until some weeks later when Lucinda whirled around the toy room while he was building up a fire. Hadley got so transfixed watching her twirl, he singed off one whole section of his left eyebrow.

"It's hopeless, you know," Bumps, the hoe boy, said when he caught Hadley watching her on her swing one day.

"Why?" Hadley wondered, for he could smell big whiffs of Sweetheart soap with every pump she made, and he was too young, as yet, to believe that anything was ever hopeless.

"Look at your hands," Bumps said. "You'd muss her up good if ever you put those grimy things on her."

"Could be I might wash 'em," Hadley said, spitting on his palm to demonstrate his plan.

"Shoot," Bumps said. "You can't get 'em clean enough for a girl like that. Unless she likes things dirty, you ain't never gonna do anything bigger than peep at her from behind this hedge."

What Hadley and Bumps didn't know back then was that Lucinda liked things dirty.

One day, while dancing the shim-sham, Lucinda broke her leg. After three days in bed, she became so bored she made the announcement that she was going to teach the servant children how to read. "I shall begin with Hadley Crump."

That afternoon, Hadley was pulled from egg-pickling and stood up half-dressed on a stool in the necessary. His momma scrubbed his face until it was sore, squeezed him into tight shoes, and sent him off to Lucinda's room, wetting his hair with a licked thumb as he went. "Be nice to Miss Lucinda," she whispered.

It was funny that she said that.

"I already learned how to read," he told Lucinda, marveling at the way her hair resembled melted butter dripping down the pillow. A lesser boy would have faked illiteracy but Hadley always bumbled lies and, anyway, it didn't occur to him to be anything but honest.

By now, he'd been at Browning House long enough to develop a taste for Lucinda's snide ways. Bumps called her Miss Fancy Pants and snickered about her devil eyes, but Hadley would rather catch a slug from Miss Fancy Pants than a kiss from any other girl. Now she wanted to watch him stutter through some baby primer like an imbecile. If only he could! "My father teached me before he left."

"Thank heavens," Lucinda said. "I hate giving lessons."

"What are we gonna do then?' he asked, praying she wouldn't send him away.

"Well," said Lucinda. "If you promise to stop looking at me like you're about to pee your britches, I might just let you join my club."

"Club?" Hadley said with an unhappy shudder, for he didn't know how to play bridge or quilt or dance cotillions and those were the only clubs he could think of.

"It's a secret club, Gladly Hadley. That means you can't tell anyone about it. Understand?"

Hadley nodded. He strongly suspected there wasn't another girl in all Catoosa who could look so buttery while ailing with a busted bone. "Does it have a name?"

"Of course, you silly boy. Readers of Violent Indefensible Lust and Evil."

"That's too long to remember."

"V.I.L.E. for short, you dummy. Anyway, it's not like we're going to have stationary. Now go and prize up that floorboard over by the window that has my boot on it."

Under the floorboard was a small cranny stuffed with two books.

"Finally," Lucinda said, snatching them from Hadley. "I didn't know how I was going get my hands on these until my leg improved." She held up the bigger of the two. "Ever read this?"

The Curly-Q title said that it was called *Anna Karenina*. Lucinda laughed. "Of course, you haven't. No decent woman would let her son look at such a thing."

"Why not?" Hadley asked, scratching at the curls his momma had spit down.

"I'll tell you why. Read this sentence here."

This was the part Hadley had been most dreading. Licking his lips, he read in a careful way, trying his best to sound schooled.

And with fury, as it were with passion, the murderer falls on the body, and drags it and hacks at it; so he covered her face and shoulders with kisses.

"Filthy, isn't it?" Lucinda sniggered.

"Is it?"

"Yes, you little nimrod. Anna Karenina is a married woman and she isn't married to the man murdering her with kisses. This is disgraceful stuff, Hadley."

"Should I put it back?"

"Not on your life. We're going to read every unsavory word of it, and there's going to be a test, too."

"But I already told you, I read just fine."

Lucinda, perhaps the world's most accomplished sigher in all the world, sighed expertly and thumped him on the forehead. "Looks like I'll have to teach you a thing or two after all, Hadley. We're gonna read until Daddy fetches you back to work, and then I'm going to let you borrow a book. *The Age of Innocence*. I want you to search through it tonight and find me the naughtiest passage you can come up with. Now hand me *Through the Looking Glass* over there."

Hadley did.

Lucinda put *Anna Karenina* inside *Through the Looking Glass*, fit the little monocle she fancied into place over her right eye, and began to read to Hadley. Mostly it seemed boring, but he enjoyed the way Lucinda said the words like she was telling him a secret.

When it was time to go, she instructed him to hide *The Age of Innocence* down the front of his trousers until he could put it somewhere safe. As it turned out, Hadley's momma had no idea the book was evil. When he took it from under the mattress later, she said, "It was nice of Miss Lucinda to let you borrow a book."

Momma had been grinning like a possum eating a yellow jacket ever since the lessons had come up. She knew, of course, that Hadley could work his way through the trickiest of Bible passages without getting tongue-tied, but she believed there was room for improvement. Looking at Lucinda's hell-born book, Momma beamed at the thought of her boy taking on such a big endeavor. Hadley was stricken with a stomach ache, owing to all that beaming, but really, the book seemed harmless enough. It was midnight before he stumbled on anything lurid.

The next afternoon he read his passage to Lucinda.

He sat bowed over, his head between his hands, staring at the hearthrug, and at the tip of the satin shoe that showed under her dress. Suddenly he knelt down and kissed the shoe.

"Hm," Lucinda said, wrapping her finger with the chain of the tiger tooth necklace her Daddy had brought from India. "Where are the bosoms and the hot caresses?"

"Archer kissed her *shoe*," Hadley said. "I would never kiss a lady's crummy old shoe. He must really like her to do that."

Lucinda looked at him like he had two heads. Then she smiled. "Hadley Crump, you dirty boy! For a downstairs domestic, you're really rather brilliant."

Encouraged by his brilliance, Hadley began staying up late, searching for just the right thing to bring to the club. His mother gave him a stack of recipe cards that had been stained when the kitchen ceiling sprung a leak. Hadley filled the cards with lines he copied for Lucinda.

After her leg healed, Hadley and Lucinda were allowed to continue meeting under the pretext of reading lessons. It was not unusual that Hadley would find a slip of violet paper on a dirty plate with something Lucinda had copied for him.

One morning, he fished a note from the puddle of honey Lucinda had left behind with the crusts of her toast. At the time they were reading *The Adventures of Tom Sawyer*, but the sticky words he read did not come from the story.

Quick, Hadley! We need a sharp knife.

Hadley was thrilled and went to the club that afternoon with a boning knife slid up his sleeve. The fun came to a stand-still when Lucinda took hold of the knife and told him to stick out his finger. "We're going to make a blood pact, just like Tom and Huck."

In Hadley's opinion, it was enough that Huck said cusses like *by jingoes* and *damn*. "We don't need to spill no blood over this, Lucinda."

"That's easy for you to say. You trust me. I, on the other hand, have no faith in you at all. Unless you're willing to make a pact that we'll keep V.I.L.E. a secret forever, I'm going to have to ask you to quit the club."

"Them boys used a needle, as I recall."

Lucinda shook the knife. "Needle-dweedle! We're not such cowards, are we?"

Hadley looked at his finger. "That knife's real sharp, Lucinda. I cut up a chicken with it yesterday."

"We wouldn't want a dull blade, would we?"

Hadley weighed the benefits of a sharp knife over a dull one. "Okay, but I'll cut my own self, if you don't mind."

She pressed the knife against his skin. "Oh, but I do mind, Hadley. Now quit your squawking and hold still."

In retrospect, this wasn't the smartest time for him to call her a Bossy Bessie, but Hadley didn't recognize that until after she cut him.

"Whoops," Lucinda said. "You're quite a bleeder, aren't you, Hadley?"

It was a nasty game, and one that Lucinda was not above taking too far. When they read *The Poison Ring*, she convinced Hadley to drink wool dye in order to prove his dedication to V.I.L.E. After that, he puked indigo for a day and a half. After that, he quit the club.

"Oh, that's a pity," Lucinda said, knotting her index finger with the chain of her tiger tooth. "And, we were just about to start *Romeo and Juliet*, too."

"I know how that story ends," Hadley said. "You can find yourself another fool."

"It was the kissing part I had in mind to try," she sighed woefully. "Oh well. I guess Bumps Bumpstead might be interested, if you're not."

"You wouldn't kiss Bumps Bumpstead." Hadley snorted.

"I'd rather kiss you."

About then, Hadley forgot all about that indigo puke. "You would?"

Lucinda shrugged. "It might be fun."

"Alright, " Hadley said. "But, no more dye-drinking."

Lucinda didn't kiss him though. She let him lie next to her on the toy room sofa, but they both had to pretend like they were dead. Even so, Hadley reckoned that holding his breath and lying on a make-shift burial vault beside Lucinda was better than nothing at all.

It occurred to him after a year or two that people must think he was very dumb. Not once did anyone question what a slow-learner Hadley appeared to be. Sometimes, he had the urge to scream out their secret, especially to his momma, who thought it pure impossibility that anyone like Lucinda would ever give a Crump any true attention. But Hadley knew he could never tell a soul about Lucinda's club, most of all his momma.

The older they got, the trickier the books for V.I.L.E. became. Lucinda told Hadley his ears turned red whenever he gave her a particularly good recipe card.

"You like that one, don't you, Hadley?" she'd laugh. "I bet you wish I'd say such things to you."

To Hadley's way of thinking, she *was* saying such things to him, and he was pretty sure she knew it too. She plunked him on the head and poked fun at his bad haircuts and red ears, but she never asked anyone else to join their club, and she never let anyone else borrow her books — not even the acceptable ones.

Not even Dickie Worther-Holms, whose father owned Worther-Holms Homes, the biggest builder of fine homes this side of the Chatahoochee. Dickie Worther-Holms was sixteen and already had a mustache and his own motor car, and Lucinda had confided that sometimes she let Dickie kiss her. Hadley was very jealous, but he was sure she'd let him kiss her too, if only he could find the right naughty passage.

One day, Spitbone, the pigman, told Hadley about a book that was so scandalous, his young wife burned it in the dutch when she caught him reading it. *Dracula*, it was called and Spitbone said there was only one store in town daring enough to sell it — Pringles Second-Hands. Hadley made up his mind right then to save his picayunes.

He was sixteen before he could afford the book *and* pay Spitbone to buy it for him. "Watch yourself with that, kid," Spitbone warned when he handed over *Dracula* wrapped in brown paper. "That book'll get you into trouble."

Hadley didn't tell Spitbone, but trouble was exactly what he hoped to get into when he read the book to Lucinda.

At first, she only glared at it like it was a shoe with dog poop stuck to the heel. They were sitting on the floor in the toy room and Lucinda had been thinking about *Ulysses* for their next selection. *Ulysses* was not even allowed in the country, she said. Lucinda had stolen it from her daddy's desk drawer.

"A monster story?" she grumbled. "Does anyone actually fornicate in this book?"

"Worse," Hadley promised. "People bite each other."

"What fun is that?" she groaned.

"I've got an idea," Hadley said. "You read from *Ulysses* and I'll read from my monster book, then we'll decide which one is more wicked."

"Alright," she consented. "But I'm skeptical."

Lucinda read first, the period-less sentences running into each other in a way that would have been annoying had Lucinda not pantomimed the action for him:

I'd let him see my garters the new ones and make him turn red looking at him seduce him I know what boys feel...

Hadley swallowed. He could well see the appeal of garters, yet he remained convinced that his was the better book.

It was a stormy day so he reached over and tugged the curtain pull, casting the room in darkness. He switched on the flashlight he'd brought along and narrowed it on the words:

I could feel the soft, shivering touch of the lips on the super sensitive skin of my throat, and the hard dents of two sharp teeth, just touching and pausing there. I closed my eyes in languorous ecstasy and waited, waited with beating heart.

When he was done, he leveled the beam on Lucinda's face. She popped her monocle. "Give me that," she said, grabbing the book. "What does it mean, Hadley?"

"It means that this girl with sharp teeth is about to drink this fellow's blood. And I think he wants her to do it."

"Hadley," she murmured in a shivery voice. "Where did you get this book?"

"Pringles. Should I read another passage?"

"No!" she cried. "I might swoon if you do."

"Really?" he said hopefully.

"The floorboards aren't safe for a book like this."

Not in all his days had Hadley ever been so proud of

himself.

Next meeting, Lucinda confessed that she could hardly read the words, they left her so breathless. "You'll have to read them to me, Hadley. But..." she said, hugging *Dracula* against herself. "I'm afraid of what will happen between us if we share such words out loud."

Hadley knew Lucinda might only be teasing. He gulped anyway. Surely, it was high time one of their wicked books inspired something wicked.

From then on, when it was dark enough, Hadley would read *Dracula* by flashlight. When it wasn't dark enough, he'd speak in a gravelly whisper, so as to keep the whole thing sinister.

On the day Harker drove his Kukri knife into the Count's throat, Hadley grew so excited he kissed Lucinda.

For years, he'd dreamed of kissing her. He could imagine himself doing it any number of ways but always, in the end, Lucinda kissed him back. Now that it was real, his lips traveled no further than the soft slope of her cheek, but Hadley kissed that cheek as though it were a fiery pair of open lips.

When it was done, Lucinda dried her face on her sleeve.

"I thought you liked this story," he said.

"I've other things in mind for us, Hadley."

"Like what?" he asked, leaning his shoulder against hers.

"Hold your horses, Hadley. This is only our first time through the book."

That night, Hadley didn't get a wink of sleep. He couldn't wait to read the book again.

Hadley's favorite character was the slang-talking American, Quincey P. Morris, and he thought the hunt for Dracula was the most exciting part of the novel.

Lucinda, however, wanted to read over and over again about Jonathan Harker's encounter with the vampire brides.

"Do you suppose he likes those women, Hadley? Or is he only afraid of them?"

"Both," Hadley said.

Lucinda fanned her face. "Fear *and* passion? At the same time?"

"And don't forget shame," Hadley reminded. "If you ask me, Harker doesn't seem very proud of himself for liking those brides."

"No wonder he goes mad."

"No wonder," Hadley agreed. "I'd rather be Quincey."

"Quincey?" Lucinda said. "No one runs their teeth languorously over Quincey's skin."

"Yeah, but Quincey has a bowie knife."

"Oh Hadley," Lucinda sighed. "You are a baby, aren't you? I'm afraid I'm going to have to show you what's really important."

That next afternoon, Lucinda stroked the back of his neck as he read. Hadley wished he could sit there until the end of time and read her every book ever written so he could feel her hand on his skin forever. When he finished the last page, he closed the book, bent forward and pressed his lips to the toe of her shoe. Slowly, fearfully, he turned his face and looked up at Lucinda.

"Read it again," she said.

Hadley celebrated his seventeenth birthday with a smooch from the new upstairs maid, a girl by the promising name of Ethel Lewse. When Lucinda spied the two locking lips, she gave Hadley a birthday card. It read:

Come to the attic at three a.m. to receive your special gift.

Hadley tip-toed up the butler's stairs at exactly five till three. He planned to act like a sleep-walker, should anyone catch him prowling about.

The attic was reached by a door with a glass knob at the end of the hall. That night, the knob glowed moongreen and seemed to pulse, as did the floor and the walls and the bedroom doors. Really, it must have been his own pulse though, because Hadley had never felt so out of his depths. With a quivery hand, he reached out and turned the knob, wondering if he was about to find a violet note telling him he was too witless to be in Lucinda's club.

Indeed, the attic looked empty. A small octagon beam of moonlight streamed across the floor. In that beam sat an old velvet lounge like the one Harker described in his journal.

"Lucinda? Are you here?"

Nothing spoke.

He went to the lounge and ran his hand over the spikes of ancient velvet. Dust puffed around his fingers.

Hadley took out his father's pocket watch. It was a few minutes after three. He sat on the lounge and swung his feet up, worrying that Lucinda had been caught trying to sneak upstairs, and that he was soon to be caught, too. There were creaks and bumps and little scratching sounds, but nothing came of them. He watched the dust motes suspiciously to see if brides would appear. Eventually, Hadley nodded off. He was lost in a dark, uneasy dream when something touched his leg.

At first, he thought it was a mouse. Then, he was sure it was Mr. Browning. Then he was sure it was Dracula.

It was Lucinda.

Her hair hung in waves around her face and her lips looked red as red can be. He was about to ask what she put on them to make them so red when he realized that she was wearing a dressing gown with nothing underneath. Her hand was on his knee.

Something hung around her neck. It twirled and

caught the moon, aiming a soft beam of powdery light smack dab in his eyes. Hadley squinted. Beneath the dreamy trail of her hand, his muscles tensed like two-by-fours. "Lay back," she said.

Hadley couldn't stop looking at Lucinda. She seemed so different.

"Don't you like me like this?" she asked.

"I like you," he said, and when she touched her mouth to his, Hadley almost wept.

"You're shaking, Hadley. Are you scared?"

Hadley wasn't scared. He longed to grab Lucinda and pull her down on the lounge with him.

"Such wicked passion," she scolded. "You ought to be ashamed."

Hadley wasn't ashamed, though. He would have married Lucinda in an instant, if that's what she wanted. But she only wanted him to want her.

Her hair tumbled down his face like tears. She twirled the tip of her tongue in the hollow of his throat. "Hadley," she said, between twirls. "You look good enough to eat...."

There was something in the bright blue lamp of her eyes that did, at last, put the fear of God in him. Quick as you please, the necklace arced past his face and tore into his neck. It was the tiger tooth. *Jesus God!* he thought. *She means to kill me for kissing Ethel.*

Lucinda's mouth slid in the blood as she tried to seal the gash with her lips. Before Hadley understood what was happening, she began to draw his blood in her mouth, sucking hard and painfully.

"Stop that," he said, pushing on her shoulder. "This isn't how it's supposed to be."

Lucinda sucked harder, as if she knew differently. "I know you," she hissed, scrapping his hair up in her fist. "You matched me breath for breath when they put their teeth on him."

"It wasn't real," he said.

"It is now."

"You're hurting me, Lucinda." His body arched against the fire, until — with one great suck — he reached the other side of Hell.

And that place wasn't Hell at all, but it's very opposite.

Hadley was in bad shape. No matter how tightly they bandaged his throat, it split open if he moved at all.

"I might die," he told her testily. It was the next day and they had gone into the smokehouse so Lucinda could try to stop the bleeding.

"Don't be so dramatic, Hadley."

"I'm being dramatic? You know, most people make love differently."

"How would you know? Anyway, we aren't most people. Oh, Hadley, just thinking about it...Have you been thinking about it?"

Heck, as if he could think of anything else.

A slant of sunlight squeezed in through the door and Hadley watched Lucinda's tongue flicker along her lip. "All this blood is making me want to do it again," she said.

"We better not," he said, but he leaned forward and kissed the spot her tongue had just wet.

Lucinda peeled back the bandage and started running her teeth up and down his neck. Hadley shook. She barely needed to pull but a few sips into her mouth before he fell on his knees and dropped once more into Black Heaven's great abyss.

That was how he thought of it, for surely the place she brought him to could not be the Pearly Gates. God did not dwell behind such a soul-wrecking act. No, Lucinda was sending him to an eviler side of Hell. And Hadley was discovering that he liked it too much to stop her.

In the following days, his neck failed to heal because neither of them could leave it be. Lucinda said she craved him, and Hadley couldn't help but respond to her with a mix of dread and ecstasy.

Eventually, things got so bad he was forced to tell his momma a complex lie about how he had fallen on a pair of garden sheers. Momma told Mr. Browning and Mr. Browning summoned Mangrove.

"The blood's got to be going somewhere," the baffled doctor said He was right. It was going into Lucinda's mouth while everyone else was asleep.

Hadley watched the little violet note spark and disappear in the grate.

Lucinda said, "I'll keep an eye on him, Mrs. Crump, and fetch you if there's trouble."

Hadley let his mother leave. He turned his cheek on the pillow and prepared to die the heady and listless death of an addict.

"No," Lucinda said. "We mustn't do it, Hadley. I will not let you die."

Hadley couldn't believe his ears. "But, if you don't want me, Lucinda, I think I'd rather be dead."

"Don't be silly, Hadley. Of course, I want you. You're the only one like me." She tucked the blanket up under his chin. "You just rest and do as the doctor says. So long as I don't drink anymore, you're sure to make a full recovery."

Hadley was weak as a noodle but managed to smile anyway. "Do you like me then, Lucinda?"

"You know I do, Hadley."

It was then that he noticed she had something hidden

behind her back. She said, "Look here, I've brought you a new book, darling. When you're feeling better, we'll read it together. Just like *Dracula*."

She twisted her monocle into place and sighed against his ear, "It's called *The Pit and Pendulum* by Edgar Allen Poe."

The Adventures of Velvet Honeybone, Girl Werewuff

Many stories have I, and this is but one...
It starts with the moon and ends with the sun.
It's about a young girl who sat under a tree.
Velvet, she's called, and Velvet is me.

I filled a twig basket with bread and black ham
And took it one day to give to my Gram.
Dressed in a cape, the color of frost
I went off in the snow and got myself lost.

In eleven short months, I was soon to be nine.
Too big to snivel or whimper or whine.
I sat by a tree to ponder my lot
And a great sneaking shadow discovered my spot.

Ham will draw trouble, as anyone knows.
Bears like to eat it. And raccoons. And crows.
I reached in my basket and offered it quick
And the great sneaking shadow gave it a lick.

Safe! You might guess, because you don't know
That ham to a beast is not good as a toe.

CAROLE LANHAM

Snapping and cracking, It broke me apart.
Sticky and torn as a strawberry tart.

Its eyes swam with Evil like fish in a can
And perhaps in there also, was some trace of a man.
And, one or the other, I'll never know which,
Brushed my ripped throat with a tender kiss.

I stared unblinking from the bed of my grave
Past the princely Moon and its howling slave,
At a shivering tree with icicles for teeth
Where upon a lone branch, clung a last violet leaf.

Shaped like a heart, it fell on my breast
And when the sun came, 'twas all that was left.
My wounds had sealed up, like it were a dream.
The beast was quite gone, the snow smooth as cream.

But hung by its hood on the bough of a pine
Was a cape the color of a Valentine.
Never pure white as it was before.
A crimson secret, ever more.

For weeks, I fed dollies and played at jacks
And the moon, as it will, began to wax
And when it was full, a terrible thing!
The brain in my head began to sting.

It itched, it burned, it shrank to a nut.
And, muscle by muscle, my strings were cut.
My skin sloughed off and underneath
Were fur-covered bones and yellowish teeth!

And, here is the part that I don't like to say
But it happened that Dempsey was over that day.
Dempsey, dear Dempsey, my cousin of four
Towering his blocks on the nursery floor.

Sweet as a dumpling, with red apple cheeks
(they'd be scrubbing them off the wallpaper for weeks)

A more mannered boy, there never will be.
I ate him like licorice, my darling Dempsey.

The Forgotten Orphan

They had a saying at the Asylum for Fatherless Children at Slough: *No child is forgotten who is loved by God.* I think Sister Madalene made it up. They also had a door at the top of a staircase that hid a knob-rattling, floor-thumping old secret. Libidinous sighs were known to slip out between the planks. Sometimes a shadow would appear in the crack underneath, its stark shape moving from side to side like a pendulum that marks something more terrible than time.

If you stood by the tree in the cotton-works yard, a pair of eyes might look back at you from the cross-shaped window at the top of Orphans' Hall, although whether or not they were human eyes was a matter of some debate. Gunstor liked to tell people that there was a torture chamber up there, and, such were the clinks and clatters that came from that place, one could almost detect within them the rubbery snap of muscles tearing under skin. Consequently, a few us were convinced we would be sent up to be stretched if ever we did something bad. Mr. Foglehorn (beetle-eyed fiend that he was) made a point of using our fears to tame us. "Step out of line with me, lads, and I'll send you up the staircase."

When I was still living in Boys B, that terrible old door

inspired many a dare. Ormsby slept all night on the bottom step once. He was supposed to sleep on the top step but, after he pissed himself, we let him move down one step at a time and the last step was where he settled. Despite the fact that he soiled his only breeches, we all thought him highly brave for it. Ormsby claimed he spent the hours listening to something pick at the lock on the other side of the door.

In the winter of my sixteenth year, I was to learn what was locked at the top of Orphan's Hall. By then, I had managed to put Slough's motto to the test in every way a boy can think of: from hiding during vespers in a butler's desk to skipping Latin lessons. Yes, we did have lessons. Our place was not as grim as others I have heard of. I doubt Mr. Dickens had us in mind when he was penning *Oliver Twist*. Then again, Slough was no Eton. Some of the staff cared for us fairly well. Others did not. We ginned cotton rather than twisting oakum like poor little Oliver. We often got more gruel when we asked for it. At the Asylum for Fatherless Children at Slough, we were loved by God, or at least, that's what they told us. I suppose that this was the main difference between me and Twist.

The words *No child is forgotten who is loved by God* were written on a banner that was periodically remade by the sisters and hung up in the dining-hall to flap in the draft. I'd been at the orphanage six years before I ever thought to question them. One day, I accompanied Mr. Stiller, the asylum's accountant, to do the banking in Charing Cross. I was to watch the horses because the hostler was choleric. At the time, I thought I might like to be a hostler myself. To this day, the memory festers inside me like a perversion that will not be cured.

Stiller was one to drink and drove off without me while I was straightening a bridle. The esteemed bankers of Cocks, Biddulph, Ridge and Co. had closed up for the evening and would not answer when I banged at the door. I walked through dark streets whispering over and over, "No child is forgotten who is loved by God." I whispered it as the rain stopped and it started to snow and icicles began to grow on my drippy parts.

I whispered it when I read the words *Inter Free Lee* and found myself staring into the dead eyes of a naked lady with a pipe hanging from the corner of her mouth. I whispered it also when the man with the nice pale tot coat offered to show me the way, then proceeded to put his tongue in my mouth. My shoes did not last the two days and nights I spent on the streets, but I held a picture in my mind of everyone at the asylum, pounding their porragers on the tables and raising a shout of praise when, at last, I found my way back.

When I found my way back, no one raised a shout. Turns out, no one even missed me.

Determined to be needed, I did time with the lardner, the millwright, and the coppice keeper before Dr. McRiffin and I finally found one another. I used to want to be a priest because Father Algernon ate like a king, but my time with McRiffin changed all that. I was hooked the first time I heard my name being shouted from so many different mouths; I could only spin like a happy little top, unable to decide where to head first. Soon, I was telling McRiffin that I might like to be a doctor myself.

Most people reared from Doc like a case of bad breath. He suffered drug disease and was either sloppy or skilled — you never knew which until he set in — so, people felt afraid. By the time we took up, he was completely morphia-addled and happy to rely on me. When Harry

Kersley got three fingers stuck in a carding machine, I held him down while the doctor sawed his hand off.

"Will you faint now, Barnabas?" Rif asked me halfway through.

"I don't think so," I said. "How would Harry manage without me?"

In order that I might be closer to the surgery, I was moved into an old dry-floor closet that smelled like old meat. Utterly ecstatic, I installed a system by which the doctor might ring me at all hours with the simple tug of a string. Ormsby and Gunstor helped in this endeavor, the former drilling holes with a pickle fork, the latter stealing a bell from the pug's parlor. McRiffin yanked that string like a whip. "Barnabas!" he'd bark. "Possible measles in Girls C. Hop hop!"

Oh, and I did. I'd hop up dressed and ready, having slept in my clothes, eager to do his bidding.

One night, he tugged the string with such a particularly sound snap, I knew I was being summoned for something big. "There's real trouble this time, Barnabas," he said.

"I'll do what I can to help," I told him.

"Even go up there?" He pointed to the top of the staircase.

I swallowed. Twice.

"What is it, Doctor? What's up there?"

The old man gazed at that door as though he gazed into the eyes of Lucifer himself. "It's a wild animal, that's what that is. And a sick one, to boot."

"I don't understand."

Rif nodded grimly. "I'm about to tell you something that no one's supposed to know. Are you up to that, Barnabas?"

He checked my face as though sincerity might be diagnosed like pox on the skin, inspecting high and low for hidden pustules of doubt. "Very well," he said. "Some fifteen years ago, Sister Madalene had a child. An ungodly child. A child not fit to live. Now the sorry thing is sick."

"But how do we know he's sick?"

"This came out with the dinner tray tonight." McRiffin handed me a note. It said: *I'm dying*.

After all I had imagined, it was difficult to believe the creature behind that door could write. Harder still to swallow was the thought of stout, stern Sister Madalene engaged in an act of passion that involved anything but rage. I liked it better when I could dream that griffins lived upstairs.

The doctor explained that the opening behind the door had recently been altered to prevent Sister Madalene's baby from escaping into the world. "The entrance is only yea-big and a man such as me could never pass through it. You, on the other hand, are squirrelly enough. I'm pretty sure you'll fit."

I squared my shoulders and raised my chin. "I'm not as small as I used to be."

He patted me on the head. "You'll fit just fine, boy. Madalene's baby, on the other hand, won't venture near the opening. It's deathly afraid of small places."

Those last words set me to shivering.

"Why would anyone lock a baby away?" I wanted to know.

"You haven't seen this baby." Another pat. "Rest assured, I wouldn't send you if I thought you'd be hurt. You're too valuable to the asylum."

That was all I needed to hear. "What do you want me to do?"

"Give it a look, nothing more. If the little beast gets violent, rap three times and I'll let you out right away."

McRiffin explained that he would need to lock me in

until I gave the signal. For *safety* purposes.

Behind the doorway was a second opening made of brick and mortar. I had to crawl in the dark through a tunnel to get to Sister Madalene's ungodly child. As I crawled, the awful thing wailed at the other end. I couldn't help but think McRiffin might have made it if only he'd let me shove him from behind.

I would have been glad to shove him from behind.

A monster waited at the end of that tunnel, judging by the sound of things. I imagined a vampire, a werewolf, or some half-man, half-dog thing that hungered for my flesh. I pictured skeleton fingers digging their way through a crumbling wall. I saw eye sockets teeming with maggots. More nights than not, a boy could hear something heavy striking against stone just above his head. It was my fear the monster would crash down into my bed one night and kill me before I got the chance to see its face. I was afraid and I knew it would be awful, but I still wanted to see its face.

I lit a match as I crept along the tunnel and, when it flared, the monster at the end made a noise rather like Kersley made when his hand came off. I dropped the match. My heart almost quit but I lit another. This time I saw something of what lived there — its feet.

They weren't bad, I must say. In fact, as far as feet go, they were boringly human and the same could be said of the legs attached to them. To see the rest, I'd have to leave the tunnel. Despite the normalness of those few parts, I still had a dread of the rest.

"I'm coming in. Don't be afraid," I warned, the words echoing in all directions like pain behind a poked eye.

I must have secretly been holding out hope that a goat

head might be attached to that body for I was, once again, left unimpressed. Unimpressed, and yet, more surprised than if an actual goat head had been fixed upon its neck.

"No!" I cried, because it seemed too horrible to be true. The creature that had terrorized our dreams and quivered our bladders and made cold sweat to trickle down our backs for all our lives was a *girl*. Worse still, she wasn't even all that ungodly. She backed away from me though, as if I were a regular oddity.

Scrambling through a pile of books, she flipped through pages in a panic. Finally, she tapped a blackened nail on a picture of Huck Finn. "Boy?" she said, thumping Huck and pointing to me.

I nodded. "That's right."

She popped a dirty finger in her mouth. "I've always wanted one."

By the time McRiffin opened the door, I nearly ran him down. "What took so long?" I said, hurrying to slam it shut behind me.

"The damned lock's stiff as a groom on his wedding night." He touched my cheek and I saw my blood on his hand when he pulled it away. "Well?" he said.

"Well what?" I answered stupidly.

"What's wrong with it? Do you know?"

"Just a few scratches, I guess."

"Not you! The beast. Is it sick? Good God, child. What happened in there?"

I was not prepared to tell that yet.

He took me to his rooms to wash up. "Looks like you've been wrestling with a thorn bush," he said. "Or a woman."

The doctor poured me a bumper of grog and I burned my throat all to Hell guzzling it down as he worked at my scratches with pickled brown paper. "Were you able to diagnose anything for me? Sister Madalene will have a fit if we can't tell her what the problem is."

"If she cares so much, why doesn't she go up there herself?"

He dropped my arm. "You haven't forgotten your promise to keep all of this mom, have you?"

I wanted to laugh. By this point, I doubted there was anyone who wanted to keep all of this Mom more than I did. "It's Quinsy, I think."

"Did you get a good look at its throat, then?"

"She isn't an 'it'. She's a girl," I said.

"Yes, well, if it's Quinsy, we'll need to treat it right away."

"Yes *we* will, won't *we*."

"Okay, Barnabas." He threw a ball of bandages at me. "Put yourself to bed. It's too soon to think about going back after all you've been through tonight."

He was right. And he was wrong.

There was no point trying to sleep. I pulled out *Swift's Disorders of the Human Body*, turned to the entry on Quinsy, and set myself down to write in my journal.

12 March, 1904

The patient is a girl, approximately fifteen years in age, suffering from tonsillitis. Swift calls for throat flannels and repeated gargles of chlorate potassium. If the doctor agrees, will administer quinine — 24 grains, and Cocaine hydrochlorate for the pain to be given over a four week treatment period.

I smiled at my work. It was quite a brilliant lie.

I didn't feel those scratches until my cheek touched the pillow. I remembered her fingers coming at my face and I squeezed my eyes shut, as if the memory might be squeezed shut, too. Behind my eyelids, I saw it all again: The greasy spots on her princess dress. The plates of rotting food. Huck Finn, with his ugly leer, poling himself down river. It was more real than the blanket I pulled over my head.

Under the blanket, her eyes watched me still, empty as the gaze of a fish. Her teeth gnashed, the sound not unlike the sound of cotton seeds being chewed by a gin. I thought of how her dress had been left unbuttoned down the back. When she went for the book, the knobs of her spine poked through the V in the fabric. All this, I noticed in those first seconds after lighting the match. Then I burned my fingers and had to scramble to light another. The third one only stayed lit long enough for me to glimpse the little savage running at me. It went out when I hit the floor.

Blind as I was, I would have sworn I wrestled with a pig. The girl grunted, snarled, and sniffed, snapping her teeth, only barely missing the more prominent pieces of me. We did a few turns around the sticky floor, bumping things and sending objects down on our heads. Glass broke and we rolled in that, too. "Boy," she grunted, churning the word out like a belch. She pinched my face, my clothes, my ears.

"Stop. Calm down," I said. "Ouch!"

We hit a table and something crashed on my skull,

almost knocking me out. "Stop!" I ordered, and her hands did stop at last... between my legs.

She was sitting on my knees just then, breathing in and out. I could hear myself breathing in and out too. Slowly, her fingers started moving again, groping me with a Braille-like thoroughness I felt helpless to combat. "Boy!" she grunted victoriously.

I remembered myself when it started to hurt, and broke free and began to search for the door. While I banged and McRiffin fought the decrepit lock, I could hear her at the other end of the tunnel. "Come back, boy. I'm not through with you yet..."

All night long she came back for me in my dreams.

I was not the most experienced boy at the Asylum for Fatherless Children at Slough. There had been only one girl in my life: Gunstor's girl, Alice. Alice had hair as black as a sweaty night and eyes like the smoke in the Lucknow opium den I'd wandered into when I was on the streets. Thanks to a newspaper clipping she kept under her pillow, she was convinced that she was the illegitimate daughter of George V. "Our nostrils are bloody identical," she'd always say.

Unfortunately, my relationship with Princess Alice was only in my imagination, but Gunstor's blood-quickening descriptions kept the affair forever fomenting in my head. This seemed the most I could hope for. Sometimes, Alice whispered spectacular things in my ear, keeping me in such a state, I had no time for noticing anyone else.

I can't help but think that things might have gone better for me upstairs if I'd had an Alice of my own.

There was nothing I wanted more in all the world than

to be ethical and doctorly and it did me no good to remind myself that I was not yet a real physician. By this point, I was so in love with being a doctor, a certificate seemed only an after-thought. I despised the thought of going back upstairs. Yet part of me was dying for another chance.

I knew McRiffin needed me if he was to keep the Father happy and, seeing how Father Algernon was willing to turn a blind eye to the old man's addiction, McRiffin dearly wanted to keep Father Algernon happy.

"I want to know why she was put in that room," I asked the next day.

We were cleaning beakers and Doc had just taken his medicine. He was always a different man after his medicine. Calm. At peace. I envied how he could go from utterly disappointed with himself to blissfully serene in the space of a few short seconds. "Isn't it obvious why she's there, boy? The child is insane."

"Yes, but was she insane from the start? Or has living in that little room driven her insane?"

A shadow crept over his eyes. "I don't like what you're implying, Barnabas."

"Why is she up there, Doctor? Is it because she's mentally ill? Or because she's the illegitimate daughter of a nun?"

"Sister Madalene says the child was always off-balanced, and I've never had reason to doubt that good woman."

"Does that good woman ever see her? Does anyone?"

McRiffin held a beaker up to the light, checking for residue. "Sister Madalene used to visit, but the child has become so violent, she's grown afraid of it."

"I can see why," I said.

"Still, if it has Quinsy, we must try to provide some relief. Are you willing to take the medicine up or not?"

Due to McRiffin's own sufferings, he always gave injections since they were less habit-forming. The doctor, believing the girl had Quinsy, wanted me to give these injections. "I'd like to send a note up first," I said. "Maybe if I explain who I am, she won't get so rattled this time."

"That's a fine idea, Barnabas. What a smart lad you are."

"What's her name?" I asked.

McRiffin took a file from his desk. Inside was a single sheet of paper. I snatched it from his fingers:

Hemsdale, Philippa Rose
Born: 1, June 1889
Breech birth.
Child was not breathing for the first five minutes of life.

That was it.

My own file was biblical by comparison. Over the course of my duties, I had found opportunity to see my records and I knew why I was an orphan.

Due to recent changes in the Poor Laws, Abraham's family can no longer afford to feed anyone in the household who is not contributing...

That was me. But at least there were five more pages covering my schooling and the arm I broke when I was the hatcheler's helper. There was the note Kersley wrote about the kind care I gave him when he lost his hand. I was able to add to my pathetic history. This girl had no history at all, not one that mattered enough to be recorded anyway.

Dear Philippa,
My name is Bram Barnabas and I am the one who came to visit you last evening. I am the doctor's dresser here at Slough and I would like to help you get better. If I come see you again,

will you promise to remain calm?
Bram Barnabas

My letter went up with some mutton tea soup and her answer came down in an empty bowl.
I promise.

This time, McRiffin vowed to keep the key in the lock should I need to make a hasty retreat. I was hopeful that daylight would make this visit go better.
It did. And it didn't.
Certainly, I could see better but this was not, in itself, much comfort. The girl was still wearing that same filthy dress and sunshine only made it appear all the more vulgar. There were food and blood stains on the skirt. She stood in front of the little cross-window so that the sun lit up her hair like an electric charge. Her eyes were about as full of expression as a pair of coal lumps on a snowman. "Hemsdale, Philippa Rose" needed to wipe her nose. Handing her my handkerchief, I suffered nausea over the fact that I had taken any amount of pleasure in feeling her hands on me.
"Boy," she said, dropping my handkerchief unused. It was only then that I began to question how this girl could possibly understand the concept of a promise.
"Bram," I said, hoping to hear her use my name.
"I'm dying," she said.
"How do you know?"
"I bleed."
"Where?" I asked, and she started to lift her dress.
I held her hands against her skirt. "But this isn't the first time, is it?"
"It stopped before, but now I'm bleeding more."

"Is there anything else?"

The furious tangle around her head bobbed and bobbed. "I huuuuuurt."

"Where?"

"In me." She pounded on her breast. "I crrrrrrry."

I smelled the same sweaty fear in that room that I smelled on myself after Stiller left me in Charing Cross.

She said, "I wannnnnnnnnnnt."

"What do you want?" I asked, ready to give her the moon.

"Braaaaaaaaaaaam," she cried.

I was in no better shape this time, even if I wasn't bleeding on the top of my skin. "Her room is a pigsty," I told the doctor. "I wish you'd come and see it." We had gone to the quadrangle because I needed air, yet I couldn't get the stench of that place out of my nose.

"I'd never get this sturdy frame of mine through such a small space," McRiffin protested, giving himself a proud pat. "How is the throat, Barnabas? That's what we went in to fix, remember? Not her housekeeping habits."

"What housekeeping habits? The girl has been raised like an animal. She was not even told of the monthly disease. We have to get her out of there just as soon as we can."

"Impossible. You said yourself she's an animal. Look what she did to you. How can you even suggest letting her out?"

"She's a fifteen year old girl. How much damage can she do?"

"Plenty, I should think." He snorted.

"I wasn't speaking of Sister Madalene's reputation. If only you'd seen her, sir, we wouldn't be having this conversation because she would already be free."

"You know nothing of mental illness, young man. There are sixty-seven children here at Slough and it's my job to protect them. We can't risk sixty-seven children for the sake of one."

"You risked me," I pointed out.

"Well, believe me, I wish now that I hadn't. Will I never hear the end of this?"

"Never," I swore.

He shook his head. "I had such high hopes for you, Barnabas."

"What does that mean?"

"It means that you will never make it as a doctor if you don't toughen up. One must recognize a lost cause when one sees one."

"That's bloody cold."

"Oh, grow up, boy. You can't help them all. Give her the quinine and forget about her."

"I don't think I can, Doctor."

He fixed me with a bleary glare. "Is she that beautiful then?"

I could have hit him. I wanted to. "It's a lie, you know. All that rot about no child being forgotten. It's a trick."

"Good Lord, what are you babbling about now, boy?"

"No child is forgotten who is loved by God. It's a rotten joke."

"Well, I don't imagine God ever forgets anyone."

"I'm sure that's of great comfort to the girl as she's sitting in her own piss."

He motioned for me to lower my voice and began speaking out of the corner of his mouth. "You're never alone, that's what it means. No matter how it looks, you're never alone."

"It's a cheat."

"No, it's not. It's better than nothing." He clapped me

on the back. "Get a grip, Barnabas, do you hear me? Or you'll end up in a little room yourself."

I was awakened the following morning by several blows to the head. "God redeem you, Barnabas! What have you done?"

McRiffin was waving a piece of paper in one hand and striking me with the other. "This came down with the breakfast dishes this morning."

Philippa bleeds for Bram.

"No wonder you've become the girl's champion. Don't you know that all lunatics are depraved?"

"She's lonely," I said. "She wants someone to visit her."

"Well, it won't be you, I can tell you that. Damn and blast. What do we do now, *Mr. I-Think-I'm-Smarter-Than-A-Real-Doctor*? Hm? Sister Madalene will have our heads if she finds out you're diddling her crazy daughter."

"I haven't done anything of the sort," I told him. "I'm just trying to help."

"Alright then, that's good. You're a fine lad, Barnabas, but I'm afraid I was picturing a baby, not an adolescent girl. Under the circumstances, your virtue would stand a better chance in a whorehouse. Why don't we sit tight while I try and think things through, eh? Meantime, there's a head lice in B with your name on it, and two cases of the skitters in the surgery. What say we forget about your girl for a while and help those others?"

I didn't forget, as the good doctor suggested. I kerosened the head lice in Boys B and gave the ailing patients in the surgery half a dipperful of castor oil mixed with half a dipperful of molasses. Then, I went back to thinking about the room at the top of the stairs. I had plans, you see. I found a book on McRiffin's shelf about the female body. I stole a bucket from the pantry and took two dresses out of the *Our Lady of the Holy Souls* donation box. I longed to know what Philippa would be like with a little human interaction.

"If you lay a finger on her, Barnabas, I swear to God you'll rue the day you ever took it in your head to doctor anyone."

These were my only instructions when I went upstairs the next day. I was to clear up Philippa's throat and get the Hell away from her.

She wasn't really sick, of course, but I headed up with my scrub brush and a syringe full of cocaine I need not ever use, and told myself I was doing the right thing. No sooner did I step through the tunnel, however, when the girl screamed like a raving Fury and wrapped her legs around me, spilling all my good intentions to the floor. "Braaaaaaaaaam!"

She said my name now like she once said "boy". Maybe, to her, they meant the same thing.

It was hard to pull her off but I distracted her with one of the dresses. Dull as it was, it looked an improvement over the other. I had also brought *Godey's Lady Book*, one half-finished bottle of Lydia Pinkham's Patent Medicine for Female Complaints, and my own King James. "You should have a look at these," I said.

She picked them up and set them down, and glanced at me to see if this was a long enough 'look'.

"No," I said. "You need to read the words." Philippa seemed clueless. "You need to send these plates back when you're done with them too. You need to clean your room and clean yourself."

She shook her head. "Don't like it."

"Well, you must. You must keep yourself clean or I won't come back anymore." This affected her more than I might have hoped.

"I want Bram."

"Then wash your face."

She still said no.

I slammed a sponge into the bucket and scrubbed her cheeks and forehead, even as she kicked. "You have to help me, Philippa. We're going to wash your hair."

Philippa clawed and wiggled and hissed, but I'll say this for it, when it was clean, her hair shone like the honey Father Algernon dabbed on his scones every evening while we were eating our peas. The girl might have almost been pretty, if only her eyes weren't so scary and her skin as pale as death.

"You look nice," I said.

Philippa stared at me, dumb as a scarecrow.

In bed that night, I thought about that look again and it turned into something different. I saw the glassy gaze a kitten wears for its mother, and the effect this had on me was one normally brought on by Alice.

By my next visit, she had liberated my Bible of all its pages and chewed up the rules of etiquette, leaving only the medical book intact. She liked the pictures. Looking at my destroyed Bible, I felt a fear for my immortal soul. I didn't know another person who would dare to tear apart God's Word like that, and yet, if ever it had failed to serve a person, it had certainly failed Phillipa. Part of me felt a certain thrill that the Good Book had not taken.

One thing had though. She'd washed. "For Bram," she said.

"What do you do all day up here?" I wanted to know. I started to sit on her bed but it didn't seem right. Alice had let me sit on her bed once while she was looking for her hat. I could hardly face Gunstor for days after. I propped myself against the table instead.

Philippa ground her teeth and stared at me in that kitten-like way. Then she took my hand and put it on her breast.

"Don't do that," I said. I put both hands behind my back, but I could still feel the softness of her against my palm. I took a deep breath. "Tell me who taught you how to read."

Philippa growled and swept the books off the table. Closing her eyes, she cupped her breast with her own hand.

I'd been reading about mental illness and knew that patients in institutions were often said to be in an *agitated sexual state*. As a matter of fact, I found myself reading that passage over and over, as though it were a recipe for Saffron Cake. My mouth even watered, un-doctorly as that sounds.

"Philippa," I said, and her eyes popped open. "Won't you tell me who taught you to read?"

She kicked the *Adventures of Huck Finn* across the room. "Sister," she snarled.

"Sister Madalene?" I said. "Does Sister visit much?"

"Philippa wanted her to hold her. Now she won't come."

"Because you wanted her to hold you?" I asked.

"Because Philippa pinched her."

"People don't like to be pinched," I said. "Is she your only visitor?"

"Father comes."

"Your father visits you?"

"Before tunnel came." My hand had fallen to my side again and she put it back on her body. This time, it took a minute to pull away.

"Pay attention," I said, as if I were saying it to her when really I was saying it to me. "What's your father's name?"

She scratched her armpit. "Algernon."

"Oh," I said. "He's not your real father, then."

"No," she said, nodding her head yes. "Philippa is not to call him Algernon and she's not to call him Papa. She is to call him Father because that's our little secret."

I understood then that our door concealed something far more dangerous than any of us ever dreamed.

Philippa slid her hand inside my shirt. "Philippa likes Bram better than Father."

Falling prey to a lunatic is rather like falling down a well; once you're over the edge, there's nothing to grab onto.

"Shhhh," she whispered. "That's our little secret."

I ought to have known all was lost when Alice stopped me in the schoolroom a few weeks later and my pulse failed to sprint. She stood so close, her hair covered me like heat. Her breath filled up my ear. "Gunstor and I have had a terrible row. Will you let me cry on your shoulder, Bram?"

"I can't," I told her, and it wasn't even hard. "I've got an injection to give."

After a full fortnight, I was growing fond of Philippa's habit of jumping on me. She licked my nose though, poor strange thing. "Bram tastes good enough to bite."

"No!" I said. "Don't bite Bram. Never bite Bram."

Her legs were wrapped around my waist and she tilted her head and stared at me, and it was almost unbearable. The sun meant less to this girl than I did. Phillipa would take me over food. Over air.

Me.

A damnable urge (not the first!) took hold, and I started to press my lips to hers. Philippa reared back.

"Is Bram going to bite Philippa?" she said.

"Certainly not. I want to give you a kiss."

Poisoned as she was by the worst of this world, Philippa retained a forgiving innocence, trust being her only mistake.

I kissed her fast. "Well?"

She smiled. She smiled and I realized I had never seen her smile before. I felt my eyes fill up with tears and I set her down. Hard. "Let's work on your hair."

"No," she said. "Philippa wants more kisses."

I knew I couldn't just kiss Philippa like I might have just kissed Alice. Kissing Philippa would be like trying to stand a boulder at the top of a steep incline and expecting it to stay there. Inside, I was saying *I better not,* even as I bent forward and kissed her again.

I was getting tired of pushing her away. "Doesn't Bram like Philippa?" she'd ask and ask. "Doesn't Bram like Philippa's hands on him?" I couldn't sleep. I couldn't eat. I wanted to tell her that I thought Bram was crazier than Philippa because Bram was in an *agitated sexual state* all the time now. But it was more than that. When she looked at me, it was like a roomful of people cheering my arrival. This seduced me better than her hands.

So, Bram embraced his monster and Philippa smacked her hand on the floor as if to say, *I knew it!* "Bram needs Philippa," she declared.

Ten minutes had passed and I found myself entangled with two skinny arms, the smutched corners of a standard-issue asylum bed sheet, various pages from Matthew, Mark, Luke and John, and one black leg of her iron bed. In the darkened room, a cross-shaped ray of light fell squarely upon her face. This time, when she smiled, my eyes filled for different reasons.

Philippa touched one of my tears and gave me a questioning look. I lifted her off me and took the Bible pages off my wet skin. I searched for my clothes.

Philippa remained sprawled on the floor, her chin propped in the cup of her hand. She watched me like I was Germanicus come to save the war. "What is Bram doing with that medicine?"

Using the snappy slip-knot McRiffin had taught me, I wrapped a tourniquet around my arm. "Bram wants to make himself feel better," I said.

○

"Did you hear the vampire this afternoon?" Gunstor asked me at supper. "It was making such a racket up there, Foglehorn has notified the zoo."

I was enjoying my pain relief and had set out to sculpt a tower of suet dumplings on my plate.

"Everyone's talking about it," Gunstor said. "Rumor has it, the thing was mating."

Sometimes, my attention would dart to where the doctor and Father Algernon stood giving me the evil eye under the *No Child is Forgotten* banner. Earlier, the doctor had informed me that Sister Madalene was considering sending Philippa to the Poor People's Home for Idiots and Lunatics. Maybe I should have felt glad about that, but instead I'd snapped and told the man that such a place would kill her.

"What do you propose, pray tell?" he said. "Shall we move her in the closet with you?"

Gunstor thought it all great fun. "I wonder if the feisty little beast is a female?" he wondered. "I'd like a piece of it if it's a girl, how about you?"

"What about Alice?" I said, caulking my creation with treacle and stabbing Gunstor's spoon in like a war flag.

"Oh, we've broken off," he said, taking back his spoon. "As if you didn't know."

McRiffin barely spoke before locking me in for the "final treatment". He snarled something when he shut the door though, something that might have been actual words, or might have simply been a snarl. He would not look at me.

Philippa wanted to look at me. Phillipa took off my clothes and crowed, "Bram is lovelier than the box." The box was a jewelry box with brass legs that sat on a chair by her bed. I think it fell on my head once.

When she was lying on the table with my hand over her mouth, it suddenly hit me what McRiffin had said.

Have fun.

I didn't think about those words again until I opened the injection case afterward. This was to be the last treatment, yet McRiffin had filled all the vials. I headed at once for the tunnel.

"Don't leave Phillipa," Philippa cried.

I pounded on the door and waited. Nothing. I told myself he'd fallen asleep. This had happened one time before.

"Stay with Phillipa," Philippa pleaded.

I banged some more. "Open up, McRiffin."

Philippa sounded excited now. "Oh! Bram has a note in his medicine," she said.

I returned to the room with a beating heart. There was

a piece of paper with my name on it wrapped around one of the vials.

    Philippa gave me an adoring look. "What does it say?"

    I held my breath as I unrolled the words...

    I will remember you to God in my prayers, Barnabas.

Biography

Carole Lanham has published twenty-four short stories and one novella since she began writing full time in 2004. Seven of her stories have received honorable mentions in Year's Best volumes, one story was short-listed for the Million Writer's Prize, and one was chosen as a Notable Story of the Year in 2008 for the Million Writer's Prize. She has won two writing contests and two of her stories made the Preliminary Ballot for the Bram Stoker award for Outstanding Achievement in a Short Story. She is also a monthly contributor at Storyteller's Unplugged. Please visit her at:

horrorhomemaker.com
carolelanham.com.

Previous Publications

'The Good Part', *Trunk Stories* (2005), *Tales of Moreauvia* (2009)

'Keepity Keep', *Fantasy Magazine* (December 2008)

'The Blue Word', *The World is Dead* (2009)

'Maxwell Treat's Museum of Torture for Young Girls and Boys', First Place Winner at On The Premises (2008)

'Friar Garden, Mister Samuel, and the Jilly Jally Butter Mints', *Thought Crime Experiments* (2009)

'The Reading Lessons', *Son and Foe*, Issue 1 (2005), Presented as a pod cast at Parade of Phantoms (2008)

'The Forgotten Orphan', *Midnight Lullabies* (2007)

Available Now:

"These tales are sharp and uncompromising, bitter and moving."

— Paul Campbell, Prism Magazine

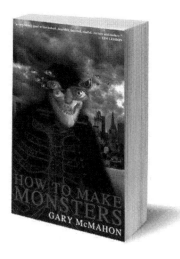

How to Make Monsters
by Gary McMahon

Since the dawn of mankind, we have always made our own monsters: the terrors of capitalism and corruption, the things between the cracks, the ghosts of self...terrible beasts of desire, debt, regret, racism...of family ties, and the things that get in the way of our aspirations...the familiar monsters of our own faces, of tradition, rejection, and the darkness that lives deep inside our own hearts...

Can you identify the component parts of your own monster?

Can you afford to pay the dreadful price of its construction?

www.morriganbooks.com

Available Now:

"*A brilliant premise of horror confined in twelve hotel rooms.*"

— Australian Horror Writers' Association

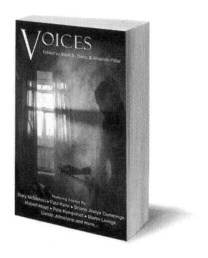

Voices
edited by Mark S. Deniz & Amanda Pillar

In every room, there is a story.

In this hotel, the stories run to the wicked and macabre.

Well crafted psychological and supernatural horror offerings await you, each written by a master storyteller. Whether you are looking to be shocked, disturbed or out-right frightened, *Voices* will have something to titillate your nerves and make your hair stand up on end. Leave the lights on and brew a strong cup of tea, the voices in the room plan on keeping you up all night.

www.morriganbooks.com

Available Now:

Dead Souls
edited by Mark S. Deniz

Before God created light, there was darkness. Even after He illuminated the world, there were shadows — shadows that allowed the darkness to fester and infect the unwary.

The tales found within *Dead Souls* explore the recesses of the soul; those people and creatures that could not escape the shadows. From the inherent cruelness of humanity to malevolent forces, *Dead Souls* explores the depths of humanity as a lesson to the ignorant, the naive and the unsuspecting.

God created light, but it is a temporary grace that will ultimately fail us, for the darkness is stronger and our souls...are truly dead.

www.morriganbooks.com

Available Now:

The Phantom Queen Awakes
edited by Mark S. Deniz & Amanda Pillar

The Phantom Queen, goddess of death, love and war, returns to strike fear into the hearts of mortals in the anthology, *The Phantom Queen Awakes*.

Meet a washerwoman on the shores of the river; cleaning the clothes of the soon-to-be-dead; try to bargain with the capricious goddess of war; hear the songs of the dead as they cry for justice; walk with heroes of the past

Revisit the world of the Celts; a land of mystical beauty, avarice, lust and war through stories told by Katharine Kerr, C.E. Murphy, Elaine Cunningham and Anya Bast, among many other talented authors.

www.morriganbooks.com

Available Now:

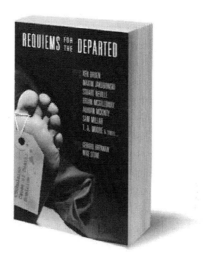

Requiems for the Departed
edited by Gerard Brennan & Mike Stone

Requiems for the Departed contains seventeen short stories, inspired by Irish mythology, from some of the finest contemporary writers in the business.

Watch the children of Conchobar return to their mischievous ways, meet ancient Celtic royalty, and follow druids and banshees as they are set loose in the new Irish underbelly, murder and mayhem on their minds.

Featuring top shelf tales by Ken Bruen, Maxim Jakubowski, Stuart Neville, Brian McGilloway, Adrian McKinty, Sam Millar, John Grant, Garry Kilworth, T.A. Moore and many more.

www.morriganbooks.com

Available Now:

Scenes from the Second Storey
edited by Amanda Pillar & Pete Kempshall

Each story in this collection has been inspired by a track from the God Machine's album of the same name. Quirky, dark, insightful and sometimes downright disturbing, these tales reflect the emotions and images our authors experienced when they heard 'their' song from *Scenes from the Second Storey*.

In *Scenes*, you will meet a girl struggling to find cleanliness in a world full of corruption with Kaaron Warren; follow the twisted mental pathways of the egocentric with Robert Hood; watch two men search for enlightenment down a dark path with Paul Haines; and dance with a girl struggling to find her role within society with Cat Sparks.

www.morriganbooks.com

Available Now:

The Iron Khan
by Liz Williams

Being considered a friend to the Emperor of Heaven has its drawbacks — especially when you're Detective Inspector Chen and the Emperor needs assistance in finding the Book; an escaped, self-aware magical artifact with the power to alter the world. Tasked with retrieving the Book before it can alter reality, Chen crosses paths with his former partner, Zhu Irzh, who is in hot pursuit of the Iron Khan, an evil, homicidal immortal intent on conquering Asia by any means.

While Chen and Zhu are otherwise occupied, Inari — Chen's demon wife — is whisked away by forces intent on revenge against Chen and ultimately, the Emperor of Heaven. The fantastical deserts of Western China and a mythical city of wonders serve as a backdrop for Chen, Zhu Irzh and Zhu's lover, Jhai Tserai, as they wage an intense, personal war to prevent their world from suffering a cataclysmic destruction.

www.morriganbooks.com

Available Now:

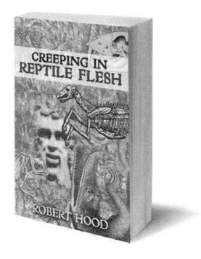

Creeping in Reptile Flesh
by Robert Hood

A detective, hired by one politician to dig up dirt on another, discovers he knows much more than he suspects…

A seemingly normal pool of water becomes a doorway for monstrous things, horrible things, hungry for human flesh…

A doctor and his "patient" discover that the location of the soul isn't in the brain, but in the heart…

This collection by Robert Hood, Australia's master of the macabre, offers 15 short stories to tantalyze your mind and tempt your appetite. From rotting food to rotting corpses, this collection is vividly thought out madness, with Hood's mastermind at its core. Leave your lights on for this one — all of them.

www.morriganbooks.com

Available Now:

"Exuberant, profane, and totally whacked out."
— Ellen Datlow, Editor

Slice of Life
by Paul Haines

Paul Haines slice through the Australian writing scene with his twisted and murderous black humor in 2002. He has since won many awards and praise for his dark and surreal stories. Paul places himself in stories that make you think twice about his sanity and good taste.

    Slice of Life boasts 17 glistening stories, sweating with 21st century paranoia and anxiety, from the decaying mind of the winter of the 2005 Ditmar for New Talent.

www.morriganbooks.com

Available Now:

Ishtar
by Deborah Biancotti, Cat Sparks and Kaaron Warren

In 'The Five Loves of Ishtar', Kaaron Warren will take you on a journey that follows the goddess Ishtar through the eyes of her most devoted worshippers, her washerwomen.

In 'And the Dead Shall Outnumber the Living', Deborah Biancotti portrays a modern-day Sydney, where male prostitutes are dying. Detective Adrienne Garner investigates the deaths, only to find rumors of strange cults and old goddesses…

In 'The Sleeping and the Dead', Cat Sparks tells of Dr Anna, who remembers little of her life before the war. When three desperate travelers rekindle slumbering memories, she begins a search that takes her to Hell and beyond. A search for love and, ultimately, enlightenment.

www.gilgameshpress.com

Made in the USA
Charleston, SC
05 October 2013